Jan wanted to talk, say anything, discuss anything, but no subject seemed properly relevant. Several times he opened his mouth to speak but always chose, at the last moment, to choke back the words.

He was excited, yes, but he was also — he admitted this — frightened. Remembering the dreadful emptiness of the timevoid, he wondered if he was prepared to endure that infinite blackness again.

He was about to tell Horatio that he couldn't go through with it when his chair began to vibrate. He looked over at the vat and saw the balls bouncing wildly. He started to scream but hastily checked that urge. He would not cry out — the others hadn't — he would be brave, too. As horrible as it was, the timevoid did not extend indefinitely. He told himself this, silently, again and again.

Then, suddenly, there was nothing around him.

And he did scream.

But nothing came out.

Then he knew he was on his way and, abruptly, without logical reason, relaxed and shut his eyes and allowed the stream of time to sweep him effortlessly and inexorably forward.

THE FIRST TWELVE
LASER BOOKS

GORDON EKLUND

serving in time

Cover
Illustration by
**KELLY
FREAS**

SERVING IN TIME

A LASER BOOK / first published 1975

© 1975 by Gordon Eklund

ISBN 0-373-72006-8

All rights reserved

LASER BOOKS are published by Harlequin Enterprises
Limited, 240 Duncan Mill Road, Don Mills, Ontario M3B 1Z4,
Canada. The Laser Books trade mark, consisting of the words
"LASER BOOKS" is registered in the Canada Trade Marks
Office, the United States Patent Office, and in other
countries.

Printed in U.S.A.

CHAPTER ONE

Lying cautiously prone on his belly, Jan Jeroux raised his chin a few inches off the stiff blanket of dry grass, then edged carefully forward on his elbows until he reached a place where the hill sloped gradually away. From here he could easily make out the wide corn field which lay directly below. Squinting against the sun, he shifted his head to see between the high stalks and counted seven, eight—no, nine figures moving between the rows. Nine, yes, and with himself that made ten. Grunting in satisfaction, he then began edging backward. If they were all down there, it meant they had given up looking for him. Just as well. The whole thing made him mad. What made them think he should be down there, too? He didn't even like to eat corn, why should he have to go and pick it?

He made his way back to the safety of a giant willow tree and slipped beneath its drooping branches. It was dark under here, and hot. He picked up the book he had been reading and laid it open on his lap, but he was still too mad to resume reading. When a person was just growing up and learning about the world in which he lived, how could anyone demand he waste his precious time wallowing in the dirt, planting and picking corn? Wasn't it boldly proclaimed right in the preamble to the Homestead Constitution that this was a free world? And didn't that therefore indicate that he, Jan Jeroux, was a free man? So what was so terribly wrong if he chose to act like one?

The question seemed to satisfy him as much as any conceivable answer, so he rolled on his side and tried to read. The hot summer sun penetrated the unmoving branches of the willow and beat against his bare back and shoulders.

The book was a chunk of old history dealing with the faraway world of the nineteenth century. Uncle Phineas had loaned Jan the volume from his vast private library. The tale told of a peculiar peasant boy named Huckleberry Finn, who ran away from his family homestead to seek the world. Jan loved the book—he had read it twice before—even though it never failed to puzzle him, too. Some of the strangeness he had managed to penetrate. Homesteads, for instance, were clearly much smaller places back then, and the world itself more savage and varied, so that running away made at least a sort of sense, because it would be different. Yet, even after numerous discussions with Uncle Phineas, some sections of the book still escaped him entirely.

For example, the part he was reading now, which dealt with Huck's visit to the Grangerford family and their feud with the Shepardsons. In one respect, this section of the book seemed most familiar to him, for the Grangerford family was not a great deal unlike the Jarman Homestead, although Uncle Phineas had pointed out that the hundred slaves owned by Colonel Grangerford should not be considered an actual part of the family unit. But the feud itself was utterly beyond him. People with guns (he had never even seen such a thing) who went around killing others for reasons even the author could not make clear.

It depressed him, too. It made him recall how, when he was young, he had thrown a rock at a sparrow for no good reason except sheer boredom and somehow the sparrow had failed to spring to flight and been struck by the rock and killed.

He remembered how Uncle Phineas had made him stand watch over the dead bird for two full days and nights as the rot of the earth crept over that poor stiff carcass.

Only then had he been permitted to bury the bird.

What was worse than that was his own guilt and remorse. It did not begin to ebb until Uncle Phineas confessed, as a boy, committing the same act and receiving the same punishment. "After that," said Phineas, "I ceased throwing rocks and you have not seen one in my hand to this day."

"Or me, either," said Jan.

And that was true, as well.

But killing people? Of all the savage acts described in antique books, that seemed to Jan not only the most shocking but also the most mysterious.

What possible reason could anyone ever have for doing such a monstrous thing as that?

A shadow fell across the pages of Jan's book. A low voice said, "Working hard, Jan?"

He glanced sheepishly past his shoulder and tried to smile. Looming over him was a huge, dark giant of a man, with a fierce black beard and small, deep eyes.

This was Uncle Phineas.

"Well, I was reading, sir."

"I didn't ask that. I asked if you were working hard."

"Oh, sure. You always told me learning was the hardest work of all. And I'm learning a lot from this book." Jan showed his uncle the cover of *Huckleberry Finn*.

"And I bet it's peaceful up here, too." Phineas crouched down beside Jan. "Hear the birds singing. The leaves swishing in the breeze. Even the grass growing. Have you ever done that, Jan? Just sat quietly and heard the grass growing?"

"No, sir, I don't think I ever have."

"And you know what strikes me as funny? It's the way nearly everything in nature grows in one sense or the other. You grow yourself, Jan, and I do myself, though in a careless, meandering fashion. Grass grows, and trees. Cows. Horses. And you know what else grows, Jan?"

Knowing exactly where this conversation was leading, Jan felt helpless to deflect it from its predestined course. "No, sir, I don't," was the best he could manage.

Phineas caught Jan firmly by the wrist and held tight. "Corn grows," he said, and hauled Jan none too gently to his feet. "And right now you're supposed to be down there making sure it stops growing."

"But, sir, don't you see that—?"

"Hush up. I don't see a thing. You lie to me and I'm not fool enough to believe it."

"But I must have forgot. Really." Jan struggled in his uncle's grip, but only because it was expected of him. He had no more chance of escaping that huge hand than a fly caught in a spider's web.

"So your sister comes to me and says where do I get off excusing you from the work detail. I say that's news to me. She says the message in the fields is that I did so. Finding me asleep, she calls me lazy and thoughtless."

"Why, I bet somebody is hoaxing us both," Jan said.

"Now look here," said Phineas, "do you ever stop lying for ten seconds?"

Jan tried to look hurt. "I started to tell you the truth, sir, but you wouldn't listen."

Phineas sighed and loosened his grip. "All right, I'm listening now."

"Well, it's this book, sir, It's something you said to me last time and has been preying on my mind ever since. I still can't figure out how Jim's situation is any different from mine."

"Because, anytime you don't like it here, you can pack up and go."

"Go where?"

"Anywhere you want."

"But there isn't anywhere to go, except other homesteads, and you know they won't accept me unless I marry into the family, and I'm not about to do that—not yet. So how can you say I'm much different from a slave?"

"Because you are. Because you happen to be one of the freest human beings who's ever lived. You may have

8

voluntarily surrendered certain past privileges in order to guarantee—"

"I never gave up anything. If it happened, you did it for me."

"Oh, Jan." Phineas groaned aloud. "All right, you win." Sighing, he released Jan and pointed to the ground. "Sit down, I have a feeling this will take a while."

Jan had that same feeling, but he repressed an urge to laugh triumphantly. Maybe Phineas knew what was up and maybe he did not, but either way the results were the same:

No work for Jan.

Phineas proceeded cogently and carefully to explain to Jan the theory underlying the establishment of the homesteads. The idea was that by peopling the earth with self-sufficient communal family farms and restricting all but the most necessary uses of technology, it was possible to provide a free and equal and livable environment for every man, woman, and child on the globe.

"You ought to read some history, Jan. You ought to find out what it was like in 1895 or 2015 before you go shooting off your mouth."

"History makes me fall asleep. I like stories better."

"Stories are fine," Phineas agreed. *"Huckleberry Finn* contains a great great deal of truth and all history can give you is mere facts. But they're important, too—facts are good to know. It's a way of growing up."

"I'm already grown," Jan said. "I'm twenty now."

"So you are," Phineas mused, "so you are. Sometimes I forget." Abruptly, he appeared to notice that it was now getting dark. He cursed softly. "We better get back home before we're lost."

Jan agreed enthusiastically. After all, what did it matter to him? The picking was long since over for the day.

By the time they reached the big house, it was more

dark than dusk and Jan could barely make out the figure of his older sister Cassie standing at the edge of the high wooden front porch. She waved eagerly in greeting. From the amount of noise emanating from the interior of the house, it seemed very likely he and Phineas were the last members of the family to return for the night.

Cassie sprang from the porch and dashed across the yard to meet them. In her hand she held a long white sheet of paper.

"Oh, Jan," she said, when she reached them. "Oh, Phineas. Something terrible has happened."

Well aware of Cassie's tendency toward exaggeration, Phineas interceded reassuringly: "There's nothing to get upset about, Cassie. Jan was out doing a favor for me and I guess I forgot to tell the work detail. I hope I caused no great inconvenience to anyone."

"I don't mean that," Cassie said. She shook the white paper meaningfully. "I mean this."

"Well, what is it, then?"

"It's not for you. It's for Jan. A messenger in a green uniform brought it about an hour ago. I didn't catch her homestead. A stranger, I think."

"A green uniform denotes a government agent," Phineas said.

"The government?" Cassie threw a hand in front of her mouth. "Oh, no."

"Let Jan have the message," Phineas said.

"I can't understand a word of it. The whole thing is—"

"Let Jan try."

Cassie nodded solemnly and handed the white paper to her brother. He held the message up to the distant light coming from the house and struggled to read. The second time through, he spoke aloud:

JAN JEROUX JARMAN HOMESTEAD SECTION 2398F AREA 78G DIVISION AH. ATTENTION: YOU HAVE BEEN ELECTED TO

SERVE IN THE UNITED WORLD CORPS.
REPORT FOR ASSIGNED SERVICE SEC-
TION 2397Q AREA 78G DIVISION AH 2400
LOCAL TIME JULY 18 2169.

"Oh, no," cried Cassie. She began to sob violently.
"Isn't it awful?"

Jan looked quizzically at Uncle Phineas: "What does
it mean?"

"Just what it says. You're going to serve in the
United World Corps."

"I figured that much out for myself." Jan spoke
loudly to be heard over Cassie's weeping. "Only, what
is it?"

"It's where your Cousin Norton went. He got that
same message fifteen years back."

"I didn't even know I had a Cousin Norton."

"That's because, after he went away, he never came
back," said Phineas.

CHAPTER TWO

On the evening of July 18 when Jan returned to the big house after work detail, Uncle Phineas was standing on the porch, waiting for him.

"I already told you," Jan said. "I'm not going."

"I remember you saying that."

"And them?" Jan pointed into the house. "What did they say? The council?"

"They voted you should go. They're scared. You can't blame them. They don't understand the world government."

"I didn't even know we had one," Jan said bitterly. "Till the message came."

"Well, don't worry about it."

"But tonight's the night."

"So what? Are you going to let a council of old folks make your decisions for you?"

"No."

"And you haven't changed your mind? You still don't intend to go?"

"I don't."

"Well, it's your choice to make. Cassie doesn't want you to, either. She made quite a plea before the council, not that any of them listened with more than half an ear. They think she's too young to have intelligent thoughts, which is backwards of the truth as well as plain stupid."

"I just wish my mother and father were here," Jan said fervently. "They'd have listened to them."

"I imagine they would have, yes. Your parents were

the sort of people, when they talked, people did indeed listen."

"Phineas, where are they?"

"I told you many times before, Jan, I don't know. That's the truth. They had to leave the homestead shortly after you were born. I know they intended to come back and, since they haven't, I can only guess their reasons are good."

"Do you think they're dead?"

"I have no idea, Jan."

A sudden, confusing thought struck him: "Phineas, did the same thing happen to them that's happening to me? Were they drafted, too?"

"Drafted?" Phineas shook his head. "No, it wasn't that."

"But—"

Phineas suddenly yawned—loudly. "It sure is a gorgeous night. I feel like some fresh air. Let's go for a walk."

"But I wanted—"

"A walk will do us both some good." Phineas started away from the big house at a brisk pace. Jan hurried to follow. Ahead of them to the left stood a high stand of evergreens, pine and spruce, and beyond that first brief hint a thick forest more than an acre deep. The forest served as a natural playground for the younger children, which was why it had been allowed to remain when the rest of the land was cleared for planting, but it was also a splendid place for taking solitary walks. Jan often came this way alone—particularly during the past few nights since the message had come.

The path they followed was sufficiently wide so that both could walk together. Between the high branches of the trees, Jan could glimpse the stars shining impersonally down. The moon, in its third quarter, had not yet risen. Phineas ignored all Jan's attempts to discuss his personal problems and finally asked him to keep quiet. A short time later, Phineas waved an expansive hand at the stars:

14

"They make a person think, don't they?"

Jan wasn't feeling especially cordial. With all his own problems, how was he supposed to have room to worry about the stars? "I don't know—do they?"

"They do me. Of course, I wouldn't know about you. Tell me, do they still teach astronomy in the school?"

"Only at the higher levels."

"Well, that's wrong. They ought to teach it to a person even before he knows how to read. It doesn't take a single word to describe any of this." He shook a fist at the stars. "It can't be done in one word or a million."

"Maybe you could bring that up at the next council meeting."

"Maybe I could. But you know my opinion. Education is falling to pot and ashes. There are times I fear we are fast becoming a race of incipient morons. Which is another risk that comes from dwelling in Utopia. People never did want to learn unless it served some practical good. The smarter a society gets, the dumber are its individual components."

Jan was hardly in the mood for listening to Phineas's philosophical mutterings. "What does any of that have to do with me?"

"Not a thing. But astronomy—now that's as relevant to any man as reading or writing or simple multiplication or learning how to use an axe. What it teaches is humility. When I was a boy, your father and I spent hours studying the stars and I think that's a primary reason why he turned to science later in life. I'm nothing but an amateur myself but I do know this: all men have an ugly tendency that leads them into developing swelled heads. They look at the earth beneath their feet and get to thinking they are the lords of creation. If they'd ever look up there—" he pointed into the sky "—they'd learn better. If they knew what they were seeing, they'd soon realize that their whole race is as petty and infinitesimal as the fleas that cluster on a dog's back. More so."

"It's just too vast for comprehension," Jan said,

sucked into the conversation despite his will. "That's the problem."

"I disagree," said Phineas. "I think it's just the right size."

"But no one person can ever hope to understand it. What else can you do except stand and stare and wonder?"

"That is my point. That is exactly what should be done. How big is the universe? I'll answer that question. The answer is, I don't know. And it's a good answer, too. All of the really important questions are always answered that way: I don't know."

"But wouldn't you like to know?"

"Sure. Who wouldn't? I'd like to know about space—about time, too. What is eternity? How did time begin? Where can it possibly end?"

"I don't know," Jan said, with a wink.

"No, that's not right," Phineas corrected. "Time and space are different."

"They are?"

"Sure. Here—sit down." Phineas pointed to a log at the edge of the path. They dropped down together. Phineas removed a cob pipe from his trouser pocket and ignited a flint lighter. "The point is," he said, "that time doesn't really have a beginning or an end. It doesn't have a middle, either. It simply is."

"I don't understand."

"No reason why you should. Let's take this particular instant right now and use it as an example. Except that you can't—because the instant is already passed. So let's pretend it isn't. Let's take it and examine it and study it and see that this instant, as it is occurring, is time— all of time. It, the instant, is past, present, and future all rolled into one, because none of those things really exists except for the one true now of the present moment. Time is not a straight line, with a definite start and finish. Rather, it is a single dot, a point, an infinitesimal pinprick.

16

"Then what you are saying is there is no past. But what if I can remember one? Am I wrong?"

"Of course not. But when are you remembering the past? Then—or now? The past, you see, is always part of the present. It exists only in the form of memory. The future, too—we call it vision or expectation or hope. Now take the stars, for instance."

Jan followed Phineas's pointing finger high into the sky.

"Take that one there—the very bright one—that is Sirius. It happens to lie something like eight light years from Earth, which means that the light we are now seeing actually left the star eight years in the past."

"Then there is a past," Jan said. "That light is it."

"So a person might think—at first. But actually that light, for us, did not even exist twelve years ago. We knew nothing about it. Now, for the creatures, if any, who reside upon Sirius's planets, that light did indeed exist then. But it doesn't now. To them, it's long since gone. So, you see, that proves my point. Everything only exists in the now—it must be considered as part of the present. You should believe in nothing else, Jan, and accept nothing else."

"Why?"

Phineas shook his head and suddenly chuckled. "A good question. But I suppose you'll find out someday. Either you will or you won't, but that'll be in the future and, as I just told you, the future doesn't really exist." He tapped his pipe against his knee, then stood up and crushed the glowing ashes. Now, without the faint light of the pipe bowl, it was nearly pitch dark.

Jan stood up, too.

Phineas seemed to hesitate. He glanced into the woods, then turned back to Jan. "But I want you to remember what I said. Will you promise me that much, Jan?"

"Yes, sir. Of course."

"Good." Phineas laid a strong hand on Jan's shoulder and kept it there for a long moment.

Then a twig snapped.

The noise, in the silence of the forest, came as loud as any explosion. Jan spun on a heel and peered between the dark trees. "Who is it? Somebody there?"

He turned back to Phineas, but nobody was there. The path was empty.

Another twig cracked.

Jan spun again. A light suddenly flared. The beam struck him square in the eyes. He was blinded. "Help!" he cried. "Uncle Phineas! Where are you?"

The light sprang closer. He heard footsteps running, too. Then he realized what it must mean: it was them—the government: they had come to get him.

Turning, he tried to run.

Another light flared from the opposite side of the path.

They had him trapped.

Rubbing his eyes, he fought to clear his sight. He saw a shadow very near and swung in defense. Hard bone cracked against his fist. A voice howled in pain.

Turning down the path, he tried to run back toward the house. It was useless. More and more of the bright lights exploded at him from every conceivable direction. At last a log tripped him. He fell flat on his face in the dirt.

Somehow he managed to stagger back to his feet. "Uncle Phineas? Where are you? Uncle—?"

Then the men were on him. Two pulled him down while a third grasped his wrist. Jan jerked loose, rolling free on the ground. He swung his fists wildly.

Then they had him again. There were more of them, and he couldn't move. His wrist was caught and something long and sharp penetrated the skin. He howled. Then, suddenly, he was laughing, too. He started to rise up into the air like a helium balloon. He couldn't stop laughing.

Then he couldn't remember anything any more.

CHAPTER THREE

Jan Jeroux burrowed snugly into the thick mattress beneath him and sighed serenely, certain he had never felt a bed quite so comfortable as this one. Waking seemed like a tragedy of grand proportions. If he could, he would gladly stay here forever. It was paradise. A golden land. No fears, no worries, nothing but the uninterrupted bliss of dreams. It was Utopia, Shangri-la.

But—if that was so—then where was it? He suddenly realized he had absolutely no idea where here was. The last thing he could recall, and that dimly, was walking through the forest with Uncle Phineas.

And then those men had come. He remembered them, too, now.

Which meant—what?

For the first time since coming awake, he opened his eyes and looked around to see where exactly he might be.

The first thing he noticed was himself: he wasn't wearing a thread of clothing; he was stark naked.

The second thing he noticed was the bed: there wasn't one. He was lying flat on the floor.

The third thing was that he was cold, miserable, and uncomfortable.

Finally, he got up off the floor, which helped. Then he looked at the room itself. It seemed to be very nearly an exact square—six paces by six. There wasn't a stick of furniture—just the floor, four walls, and the ceiling. In one wall, heavy black curtains were drawn across what might have been a window. But that was the only dim attempt at human decoration. The walls were painted a dull shade of white. The floor—which he had thought so soft and comfortable—seemed to be made of concrete.

And there were two doors.

Jan hurried over and tried the first. It opened easily enough but revealed nothing beyond a rather ordinary, though clean, bathroom.

So he went and tried the second door.

This one was locked. The knob refused even to budge. Frustrated, Jan tugged and strained. Nothing happened. Making a fist, he pounded vigorously. Still nothing. So he kicked the door.

"Ouch!"

He backed away, cursing. He had forgotten they had left him barefooted along with everything else.

Turning back to the center of the room, he noticed the presence of a pile of clothing near the place where he had originally been lying.

He knew that clothing hadn't been there before.

First, he carefully scanned the walls and floor in search of some sort of trapdoor. Failing that, he went over to the pile of clothing. He inspected the various garments: there were socks, boots, underwear, gloves, pants, and a shirt. He dressed in the underwear and socks to guard against the chill. The rest he ignored. He would rather die of the cold than wear their uniform. Both the shirt and pants were bright green. On the pocket of the shirt, a patch had been attached: a white clock with no dials. He didn't know what that meant, but he didn't like it, either.

There seemed nowhere else to look—nothing else to inspect—but the window. He went over there and cautiously parted the curtains. The glass behind seemed so black he thought at first it must be painted.

Squinting, pressing his nose against the dark glass, he strained to peer through.

Then, seeing, he reeled, almost falling, and quickly shut his eyes.

He had seen nothing out there. It was dark—no, not dark, for he could have withstood that; it was black

20

out there. Pitch, total blackness. Not a hint of light. Not a shade or a shadow. Just utter, impenetrable blackness sweeping in every possible direction.

He made another determined effort to look but his senses rebelled at the ghastly sight they were forced to endure.

Again, he backed off, swaying dizzily.

It was no use. With a shiver, he drew the curtains shut and turned away.

The room had changed again. His nose told him so. He sniffed food, so he looked. A plate of real lamb chops sat on the floor beside the remaining pile of clothing.

He couldn't resist that. He was hungry—and weak. To eat, he used his fingers; no utensils had been provided. The meat turned out to be delicious—far juicier than what he was used to.

When he finished, he sat back and patted his belly with satisfaction. Sooner or later somebody would be coming for him.

When they did, he intended to be ready.

He was dozing upon the floor when the first man entered.

At the sound of the door closing, he immediately awoke.

The man was small, fragile in appearance, and dressed all in green. He wore wide round spectacles and might have been sixty or seventy years old.

The man approached Jan with his right hand extended in greeting.

Jan sprang to his feet. Unhesitantly, he threw a long left hook. The blow connected. The little man's spectacles flew off his face, shattering against the floor. The man stared at Jan, his mouth hanging open in apparent horror.

Jan swung at him again, but his fist fell short. A sharp, sweet odor tickled his nostrils. He felt sleepy again.

Then he was asleep.

21

He was just finishing his third plate of lamb chops when the door opened quickly and a man stepped through. This representative was wholly unlike the first man. He was huge, gigantic, and glowering. He marched toward Jan with steady, certain steps. He was dressed all in green and carried himself with military rigidity.

Jan came cautiously to his feet.

The man stopped a few paces short of Jan. He shook an angry finger: "I've come here to tell you a few things, boy. You want to listen to me or not?"

"I want to go home," Jan said. "I've been kidnapped against my will. That's against the law."

"Here we make the laws, not you. This is your home from now on. You can forget about that other place."

Glimpsing no prospect of hope in the man's words, Jan shrugged. "Okay—then I guess I'll listen." He dropped his arms casually to his sides.

"To begin with—" the man began.

Then Jan hit him with a left hook.

The blow struck neat and clean and swift. Unfortunately, it appeared to have no effect whatsoever upon its intended victim.

The big man blinked, grunted, licked his lips. Without a word, he swung at Jan. His fist sailed through the air like a massive hammer. Jan's paltry defenses were as useless as a barricade formed of wet paper. The blow struck him squarely on the right cheekbone and he crumpled.

The man glared down at Jan, who lay motionlessly upon the floor. "Ready to listen yet?"

"Sure," Jan muttered. Slowly, he struggled to his feet. Once there, he swung.

This time the big man ducked, dipped, and bobbed upright. He struck in return without hesitation.

Jan hit the floor hard and bounced off.

"Want to listen?"

Jan nodded weakly. Pushing up with his hands, he staggered to his feet. He swayed, swung, and missed connecting by several feet.

Crack. He hit the floor again.

This time he didn't get back up.

When he regained consciousness, the following portions of Jan's anatomy either ached or stung or both: the jaw, nose, eyes, cheekbone, forehead, mouth, chest, arms, abdomen, stomach, knees, ankles, feet, toes, and buttocks.

Groaning with the vastness of this suffering, he somehow managed to squeeze both eyes open.

He was in the room on the floor, with a plate of food in front of him.

His stomach revolted at the sight and he tilted his head painstakingly away.

Then he saw the girl. She was young, tall, and perhaps pretty. The latter was difficult to know because her face was painted in a macabre fashion suggestive of the graveyard: lips streaked red, eyes shadowed black, cheeks smeared white.

He shuddered at the sight of her and briefly wondered: *Heaven? Could I be there already? Is this an angel?*

But her words convinced him she was merely human: "You are really an idiot, aren't you? Throwing a punch at Mallory? You're lucky he didn't murder you on your feet."

Jan assumed Mallory must be the second, bigger man. "He nearly did."

The girl laughed. "And Whitlow, too? Don't you know he has eighty percent of the say whether you graduate from the Academy or not? I think he's too big a man to bear grudges against people just because they're stupid, but I'm not sure you even deserve that much."

"Who are you?" Jan was finding talking easier than he had anticipated. As long as he paused between every word to lick his lips and catch his breath, he seemed able to manage as many as three words at a time.

"My name is Gail Conrad. Whitlow and Mallory

asked me to pop in here and see if you were really as crazy as you were acting. I'm a trainee, too, the same as you, so you don't have to try to punch me unless you really want. Of course, I'm an expert in all forms of combat and would have no trouble beating you into a mess of bloody pulp."

"No, thanks," Jan said. "I've been turned into bloody pulp enough for one day."

"Then you really aren't crazy?"

Jan wasn't too sure how he ought to answer that: "I want to go home. That's all."

Gail laughed. "I'd call that pretty crazy." But she shrugged. "Still, everybody has a right to hold an opinion."

"Then how about you telling me your opinion? Where in the world are we?"

"Well, not in the world for one thing. But do you really mean to say you don't know any of it?"

"All I know is that some men kidnapped me. The United World Corps. They want me in it, but I don't know what it is."

Gail was shaking her head. "Whitlow told me that, but I couldn't understand it. If you don't know anything, why did they choose you for the draft? I was picked because my father and grandfather before me were corpsmen. That's usually the way it has to be."

"Well, I had a cousin. Norton his name was. My uncle said they took him, too, years ago. He never came back."

She shrugged. "Neither will you."

Jan felt his anger and frustration building again, but he was too much in pain to try fighting. He sought to remain calm: "Why don't you just tell me? All at once? Instead of letting it out in little trickles."

"I guess you're right. Here—" she held up her fingers and ticked off the points as she proceeded "—first, never call it the United World Corps. That's a front name. We call it the time corps. Second, you're a time technician in training here at the Corps Academy. You will be expected to pass a rigorous course of study, after which you will be sent into the field. Thirdly, and I guess this really should have come first, what the time corps does, its purpose, is to travel into the past. We do scholarly research, probing around, that sort of thing. It doesn't sound all that exciting when you reduce it to words, but I'm not lying when I say you're awfully lucky to be here."

But Jan didn't feel the least bit lucky. All he could do was shake his head in total dismay. He hardly knew where to begin. The best he could manage was to repeat the most incredible fact of all: "Did you say travel in time?"

"Of course. The Lackland Process. Sidney Lackland. You really didn't even know about that?"

"No," Jan said, feeling abashed in spite of himself. I—"

"They sure made a mistake in picking you," Gail said. "Wow, did they ever."

"I didn't say I couldn't do it. I just said I didn't see any real need to go traveling into the future."

Gail hooted. "Can't you even listen? I didn't say future—I said past. Nobody can travel into the future because it hasn't happened yet."

"Then all you do is visit the past? You stay there?"

"That's right."

"Forever."

"Well, at least until you retire."

"And when is that?"

"Oh, when you're seventy, eighty, no one rushes you. We've still got squad leaders in the field who were with the original corps."

This made up Jan's mind for him. He said firmly, "Not me."

Gail seemed more genuinely disturbed than ever before. "You can't mean that. Just think of the possibilities: the Roman Empire, Egypt of the Pharaohs, the court of Kublai Khan, Inca Cuzo, Byzantine Constantinople, the London of Dickens, frontier America.

Anywhere and anywhen you desire. What more could you ever want?"

"There's only one place I want to be," Jan said. "That's the Jarman Homestead in the year 2169."

Her expression radiated a deep contempt. "In other words, you want to quit the corps."

"I want to go home."

"Same thing. So I may as well tell you. Whitlow said I might have to but I didn't believe anybody could be that dumb. Well, I was wrong. You know what happens to quitters here? Have you noticed that window over there in the wall?"

Jan nodded tensely. "I tried to look out it."

"Good, because that makes it easier to explain. That window happens to look out on what is called the time-void. It is a portion of the physical universe that exists outside of time. It is used by the corps as a vehicle for traveling from one time to another. This academy has been built smack in the middle of it. If you quit the corps or if later you are busted from training, then out there is where you go. It's cruel but it's necessary. The corps cannot afford to have possibly disloyal former corpsmen walking around free with all sorts of explosive knowledge at their disposal."

"Why not?" Jan said.

But Gail seemed to recognize the question as mere diversion and she chose to ignore it. "So the choice is strictly yours, Jeroux. You can elect to stay here and attend classes and maybe even graduate from the Academy. Or you can quit—and out you go."

Jan believed her. He did not think her threat was shear bluff. They had kidnapped him. Whatever was outside that window—timevoid or not—was surely real. These were serious people. "Do you want me to say it?"

She nodded and grinned nastily: "That might be fun."

"Then I'm staying," Jan said.

CHAPTER FOUR

"All right," Mallory said, stepping away from the open door. He raised an arm above his head and let it drop swiftly, like an axe. "Second squad—get in there."

These casual words struck Jan like a painful blow to the body, but his feet were too well-trained by this time to resist, and he ended up moving obediently forward in line with his classmates. The file of green-suited trainees passed through the open door and entered the small dark room beyond. Four neat rows of folding chairs had been crammed into the limited space between the stage and the door. Jan's squad occupied the second row. At a signal from Whitlow, who stood upon the stage, they sat down in unison. None relaxed. They all sat stiffly, at attention, hands on knees, spines not touching the backs of their chairs.

Jan himself might have been trembling. Whitlow kept flashing him puzzled looks. He didn't care. If he was trembling, there was good reason for it. Today was graduation day—and Jan Jeroux was frightened for his life.

The stage was nearly as crowded as the floor. Jan tried to focus his attention up there. He saw various administrators, functionaries, and instructors. The Captain himself, head of the entire time corps, sat rigidly in the center of everyone. Jan had only seen the Captain twice before, but even this rare sight could not wholly draw his attention away from his private fears.

Would he make it? Would he fail? Would he die? These were the only questions worth asking. Un-

27

fortunately, none of them had as yet been provided with an answer.

The Captain seemed to be looking at Jan, studying him, but when Jan tried to meet his eyes in hopes of discovering some form of reassurance lurking there, the Captain looked quickly away.

He knows, Jan thought. *That's why he can't meet my eye. He knows I failed and that I'm going to die.*

It had taken Jan two full months to reach this predicament. Two dreadful months of teaching, learning, studying, testing, and failing. The history of the ancient world; European civilization; the Americas; Russia; Chinese history; political history; military history; cultural history. And on and on and on. History, history, history—facts, facts, facts. His mind had become so saturated with details of the dead world that, by the time of the final examination, he had suffered enormously trying to recall who was who and what was what. It hadn't been fair. He was convinced of that. If he failed and died, his death would be a stain upon their hands. Not his own. The blame and guilt would be theirs to bear.

The third squad was now filing into the room. One more to go and the entire class would be present and waiting. Jan moved his eyes down the row seated in front of him. Although he couldn't see any of their faces, he knew each one of them simply from the back of his or her neck. He knew them that well—better, in some respects, than his own family. Altogether there were thirty-nine in the class. In the beginning, there had been forty, but one boy had dared to risk quitting after a poor first exam, and no one had seen a sign of him since. Thirty-two of those remaining were boys. They shared a common barracks, as did the seven girls. The oldest of the boys, a former teacher named Arthur Dodge, was actually a full-grown man, in his late thirties. But most of the rest—and all of the girls—were in their teens or very early twenties. Jan had no particular friend among their ranks, or any real enemy, either.

28

He felt he got along with them all equally well.

There was one exception to this.

The exception presently sat, as squad leader, at the end of Jan's second row. Her name was Gail Conrad and he was beginning to believe he actually hated her. As leader of his squad, she was in the perfect position to pay him back for what she apparently considered his lack of loyalty. In the last two months, she had done her best to make life utterly miserable for Jan. Evenings he should have spent studying with the others were instead devoted, at Gail's direction, to scrubbing pots and cleaning sinks and washing clothes and dishes. Out of this had come Jan's favorite dream. Every night when he fell asleep, he wished for it to come. In this dream, it was graduation day. The class rankings were announced and there at the very top stood Jan Jeroux. Gail, poor Gail, there she was at the bottom—a certified failure doomed to awful extinction in the nothingness of the timevoid. Unfortunately, the whole dream was pure fantasy. If in the cold reality of today Gail failed to attain top ranking, it would be an event rivaling in remarkability the original invention of the time traveling process by Lackland. Gail had known more than enough before ever reaching the Academy to pass the course.

In fact, this was one point which struck Jan as most unfair. Nearly all of his classmates seemed to be the sons and daughters or brothers and nephews of men and women already enrolled in the corps. One of Whitlow's daughters had graduated in the class just ahead of Jan's. The best he could manage was the long forgotten Cousin Norton. The others had learned first-hand about history in their parents' laps. They were as familiar with Napoleon and Einstein and John Hancock as he was with how to hoe weeds or pick corn. One thing it wasn't and that was fair.

The boy sitting to Jan's right—his name was Kirk Rayburn—suddenly muttered aloud, "If I don't make it, I'm going to fight."

Jan glanced around to make sure no one was watching them, then whispered: "Me, too."

"In fact," said Kirk, "if they try, they'll just have to kill me to my face. I'm not going out there of my own will."

"Me, either," said Jan.

"If I have to, I'll take a couple of them with me. Mallory, for instance. Wouldn't you love to take care of him, Jan?"

"You bet," Jan smiled at the thought. Kirk Rayburn was Gail's particular favorite within the squad and Jan had never quite trusted him as a result, but sometimes he did come up with a good idea or two. "Leave him for me. I'll——"

"Shut up down there, Jeroux. You're supposed to be seated at attention." Gail Conrad's voice lashed through the room like a knot in the end of a whip.

Jan faced front, muttering to himself. He could have killed her right now. The Captain, Whitlow, everyone seemed to be staring right at him. He flushed and tried to keep calm.

But just at that moment, the Captain suddenly rose from his chair and stepped forward. In a soft but firm voice that was barely audible, he said, "Ladies and gentlemen, you may sit at ease."

Jan dropped his hands into his lap along with the others.

"Whitlow, come here," the Captain said. "You've got the list?"

"Yes, sir," Whitlow said. He approached the Captain, a long sheet of parchment clearly visible in his right hand.

"Well, let me have it."

"Of course, sir."

Jan watched the passage of the parchment from hand to hand, very much aware that his fate—his life—hung in the balance.

Whitlow stepped back. The Captain raised the list, seemed to study it, then announced, "I am going to read your names in the order in which you have finished. You should all be aware that class ranking has little or no effect upon future assignments or promotions. If your name is not announced, it means you have not graduated. Are there any questions?"

Of course there were none. The moment had long since passed when any question might have been pertinent.

The Captain spoke:

"Gail Conrad."

Whitlow beamed down at his favorite pupil—he had never forgiven Jan for punching him that first day— but if Gail herself was at all moved she failed to show it.

"Arthur Dodge," said the Captain. Dodge was the professional historian—no surprise there.

"Jason Clarke," was the third name read.

Then came: "Leonard Walters."

The tenth name spoken by the Captain was: "Mary Norwood."

Then came the eleventh name . . . the twelfth. Numbers thirteen, fourteen, and fifteen.

When the twentieth name—Kirk Rayburn—was announced Jan ceased counting. It was more than half-way over. That was terrible enough to know.

Yet name continued to follow name. Everyone gasped in relief. A few dared to cheer. One very young boy— Barry Reynolds—actually broke down and cried. Jan refused to blame him. Right now, he felt very much like doing the same. He didn't want to die—not here, in this place. He wanted to see his home again.

The Captain read another name. It wasn't Jan's.

It seemed to him far more than thirty-nine names had already been uttered. Maybe the Captain, deviously, was reading them over a second time to extend the torture.

Then the Captain said, "And Jan Jeroux."

After that, he turned quickly and walked back to hand the list to Whitlow.

Jan sat, too stunned to gasp or shriek or wail or cry

or faint or groan or howl. He had passed! How about that? Passed!

It was all over. He was last—but alive.

Then, in the row immediately behind Jan's, someone screamed. This was not a cry of relief or joy. Rather, this came from sheer terror.

Jan spun around to see.

It was Albert Mitchum, a boy barely sixteen, who had claimed seven generations of corps descent before Gail informed him the Lackland Process was barely fifty years old. Mitchum was standing upon the seat of his chair. He shook his fists at the stage:

"You're liars! It isn't true! I passed—I know I did! You cheated me!"

Nobody else made a sound or budged an inch or raised a protest.

Then Mitchum sprang off the chair and rushed the stage. He seemed to be attacking at random, lashing out toward no one in particular.

But it was the Captain who stepped forward to intercept him. From his belt, the Captain pulled a tiny silver object, with a needle-point tip. Could this be the gun the old books described? Jan didn't think so. Actually, he thought it was the same weapon those men had used on him the night he was kidnapped.

Mitchum threw a wild punch at the Captain, who ducked with amazing dexterity, and slapped his hand gently against Mitchum's spine.

Instantaneously, as if struck by some supernatural force from heavens, Mitchum went stiff and rigid and then collapsed on his face at the edge of the stage.

Then everything went into motion. The class—including Jan—jumped from their seats and rushed the stage. Gail shouted into the bedlam for them to get back. Mallory cried out, too. But no one was stopping.

Then the Captain's voice, no louder than before, rose easily above the clamor: "Now step back. Please. No closer. Give this boy air to breathe."

"You murdered him!" shouted an anonymous voice from within the mob of trainees.

"Oh, he's not dead. You needn't worry. Merely stunned. He'll be awake in forty moments."

Jan stepped obediently back with the others and took his seat. The Captain was bent down over Mitchum's body, administering some form of first aid with his fingers.

Then Jan laughed. His high, shrill voice cracked the tense silence that now presided over the chamber. *Not dead,* he was thinking. That was what struck him as funny.

Poor Mitchum. Not dead now—no. But when, how soon, how very soon he would be.

Poor Mitchum had, after all, flunked the course.

CHAPTER FIVE

Out of breath from his long dash through the Academy corridors, Jan shoved the green valise containing all his worldly possessions beneath a chair, then collapsed into the empty seat between Kirk Rayburn and Arthur Dodge.

"Anything happen yet?" he managed, after a struggle for sufficient air. "I'm not too late?"

"If you are," Kirk said, "it doesn't much matter. I got here twenty minutes ago and there hasn't been a peep out of them."

"If somebody doesn't do something pretty soon," Arthur Dodge said, "I think I'll jump on top of this chair and scream at the top of my lungs. Sometimes I think they're sadists the way they make us wait without explanation. Sometimes I really do."

"Whitlow here?" Jan said.

"Yeah. And Mallory, Cox, Sullivan. The whole works except for the Captain, who probably collapsed after all the exercise he put in." Kirk jerked his head toward a thick steel door in the opposite wall. "They're huddled in there."

"What is it?"

Arthur answered in a voice heavily laden with awe: "The Lackland Process."

"The time machine?" Kirk seemed to ponder the idea. "How do you know that?"

"I was here before," Arthur said. "When I was a teacher."

"Then you traveled through time before, too?" Jan said.

35

"Only once. Just that one time about a year ago. But it was—it was unbelievable. It made me realize how silly it was for me to study books and other records and think that was history." It was well-known among the students that Arthur Dodge had pulled strings in order to get into the Academy. At his age, he rightly should never have been considered.

Jan, Kirk, and Arthur, along with their thirty-five surviving classmates, were seated in a big, barren room somewhere near the center of the Academy complex. Jan was the last of the class to arrive. After the completion of the graduation ceremony, everyone had been granted exactly one hour in which to gather and pack everything they owned and report to this location for what was described as final processing. Whitlow had further cautioned that no one should eat or drink or smoke until given an order to the contrary. Jan had seen only one possible way to interpret this: it meant there would be no waiting; they were going downstream right now.

"What took you so long, anyway?" Kirk asked.

"Oh, I stopped and cleaned up Mitchum's area. He brought an awful lot of junk with him—pictures of his family and everything. He was a Homestead kid, like me, so I guess I felt an obligation."

"That's not what he told me," Arthur said, clearly puzzled by the contradiction. "He told me his father was a squad leader in seventeenth century India."

Kirk laughed. "Oh, that crap. He had a different story for everybody. Weren't you there the night Gail finally shut him up? He darn near cried. It was really funny."

"No, I missed that," Arthur said.

"Too bad." Kirk turned back to Jan. "So what happened to all the junk? Did the Captain get it?"

"No, the matron said they'd return it to his family."

"Oh, I bet they'll be pleased to get that. It's a wonder they don't ship them his head, too."

Jan did not feel like discussing the subject any

further. In fact, he was sorry he had brought it up at all. Why had he even done it? He could tell that Kirk thought he was soft for doing so. The best answer he had been able to give himself was that he had done it because it was appropriate that he should. Why had Mitchum failed when he had not? What if the line had been drawn one name higher? What if Mitchum, guessing at a particular answer, had been lucky, while Jan, guessing at that same answer, had not. The border between life and death seemed far too thin to Jan. It was easier to sympathize with a loser when one was not wholly a winner himself.

In the barracks, Gail had briefly tried to stop him from packing Mitchum's goods, but when Jan threatened her with a fist, she apologized. Actually Jan thought Gail probably understood what he was doing and why better than someone like Kirk, or even Arthur. He might not like her, but she was far from being a fool.

"Look over there," murmured Kirk, pointing at Gail across the room as though he had been listening in on the flow of Jan's thoughts. "I don't think she has yet figured out that she's nothing any more."

"Somebody has to take charge." Gail was moving around her former squad members and ordering each to open his valise so that she could inspect the contents. As they watched, she sent one boy scurrying back to the barracks after some forgotten essential.

Kirk shrugged. "Then why her? It should be you."

"Me?" Jan laughed. "I was last in the class."

"So what? That just means she knows a lot about history. The only reason she's squad leader is because she's Whitlow's pet, he knew her father."

"I didn't know that."

"Yeah, they served together in time. Gail's father was killed on a voyage and of course her grandfather was right with Lackland in the beginning. The Captain was there, too. But big deal, I say."

"Sure," Jan agreed. Then someone coughed. He

looked over and saw Gail Conrad standing in front of Arthur. She had his valise in her hands and was now glaring at Jan.

"Let me see your bag, Jeroux," she said.

Jan could feel Kirk's eyes on him. Without really thinking, he said, "I didn't forget anything."

She bent down to reach under his chair. "Well, just let me see."

Jan beat her to the valise. He clutched it tightly in his hands. "No," he said, firmly.

Gail backed off. Her face registered no particular expression. She could have been shocked, amused, or angry. "Are you deliberately disobeying my order?" she asked, flatly.

"No," Jan said.

"If so, I must warn you that such an action is punishable under regulation 49 by immediate bust or, if occurring in the field, by death."

"It wasn't an order. You have no authority over me any more."

Arthur was open-mouthed at the confrontation. The corners of his mouth kept twisting as if he wanted to smile. Suddenly, Jan was resentful. Why hadn't she asked Kirk first? This whole thing was his idea. What if he was wrong and Gail was right?

"I'm your squad leader," she said. "Therefore—"

"No," Jan said, keeping his voice deliberately under control, attempting to match Gail's tone. He didn't want to attract any unnecessary attention that might force them to say or do things they would later regret. "We've all graduated, so we're all equals."

"I'm going to repeat my order," Gail said. "Arthur, you will be a witness. Kirk, you watch this, too."

"Yes, Gail."

She faced Jan with her hands balanced on her hips. "Jeroux, give me that bag."

"No," he said firmly.

She nodded briskly: "Then consider yourself under arrest. I will be right back." Turning sharply away, she headed straight for the big steel door across the room. Throwing it open, she hurried through and slammed it shut behind. Through the brief opening, Jan had glimpsed Whitlow and Mallory seated at a high desk piled with papers.

"Jan, have you gone crazy?" Arthur said.

"No, he hasn't," said Kirk. "He was right. I could have told you that."

"You might have told her, too," Jan said bitterly.

But Gail only gave him a few moments in which to worry over the possibility that he had just instituted his own death warrant. She came back through the steel door in a swift flash of motion and skidded to a halt in front of Kirk.

"Would you mind letting me look inside your valise?" she asked him.

"Of course, Gail," he said.

But Jan didn't intend to let her off that easily. "Is that an order?" he asked her.

Gail ignored his remark. She told Kirk, "We think it's a good idea to doublecheck each other."

"Oh, I agree completely," Kirk said.

Jan leaned back in his own chair and let out a deep, soulful sigh of relief.

They had to wait another full hour. In that time, Jan handed Arthur his valise and asked him to doublecheck its contents. A tube of tooth decay preventative was missing, so Jan had to rush back to the barracks to fetch one.

When he returned, everyone seemed even more restless than before. A card game was started and Jan joined in.

He had just won his first hand and was scooping up the pot when Whitlow abruptly emerged from the room behind the steel door. He held a sheet of paper in his hands and swiftly called out two names.

The people called followed him into the room and the door was shut.

Kirk, who was following the progress of the card game over Jan's shoulder said, "This is the end of it."

"The faster, the better," Jan agreed. He threw away a bad hand of cards and stood up.

"Arthur says it's in there," Kirk said.

"Yeah, but I wonder if—"

The lights in the ceiling suddenly flickered. From the other side of the steel door, a high whirring hum erupted.

It was over almost as soon as it had begun.

Kirk snapped his fingers. "That was it—they're gone."

Jan could only nod. So this was finally it—the very end. In a few moments, one thing would at last be true: he would be past the point where he might seriously hope ever to see the Jarman Homestead again.

Whitlow returned alone. He called out three more names. One of these—a girl named Mary Norwood—hung back. Jan thought he glimpsed the presence of real tears on her cheeks. He could have kissed her for that. It meant he wasn't alone here. At least one other person, like himself, had something worth losing.

But Mary Norton paused only briefly. She followed Whitlow through the steel door. It clanged shut.

A few moments later, the lights flickered. The hum erupted.

Then it was over.

"Five down and out," Kirk said.

Whitlow reappeared and called another group of three.

"I thought," Jan said, when the latest eruption of humming had passed, "there were four corpsmen in each field squad."

"Sure," said Kirk, "but you don't think four of us could survive back there for more than a couple of hours. No, there'll be an experienced corpsman or two waiting for each of us."

This time when Whitlow materialized he called out: "Jan Jeroux, Arthur Dodge, Gail Conrad."

40

Kirk slapped Jan on the back, laughing. "How about that?" he cried.

All Jan could do was moan miserably. Not her—not Gail. Why, it just wasn't fair.

Whitlow repeated: Jan Jeroux."

Stiffly, he made his feet move forward. He tried to hold his head high. At the door, he nearly ran into Gail.

She flashed him a sarcastic smile. "Don't worry, I'll take good care of you. I won't let you get hurt."

"Oh, shut up," he said.

She laughed and bowed swiftly past him.

In her wake, Jan entered the back room. Arthur was already present. He looked at Jan and seemed to wink, whether from nervousness or joy Jan could not tell.

Mallory occupied the desk Jan had glimpsed earlier. He glared at the three of them from beneath heavy eyebrows. "What a bunch," he said, ambiguously. Then he pointed at three large leather chairs that sat on the opposite side of the room out of sight of the door. "Have a seat."

Jan, Arthur, and Gail went over and sat down. Whitlow followed after them, while Mallory continued to scribble furiously at the desk.

"I'm supposed to tell you the details of your assignment," Whitlow said, "but there really isn't a great deal I can say that you won't learn better after you arrive. You're going to a place generally known as the United States of America. Your term of service will run from 1700 to 2099. Base camp has been established in the year 1729 in a place called Wyoming. Your field squad leader will be your immediate superior from here on out. Any questions?"

All three of them shook their heads. Gail looked complacent and satisfied as if she had just won a huge pot at cards. Arthur seemed disappointed and sad—Jan knew his specialized period of interest was medieval Japan, a long trip from the so-called U.S.A. Jan didn't know how he, himself, looked—but he felt scared.

Then the chair came alive. Thick leather belts sprang forth from the lining and caught his wrists, legs, and ankles in a tight grip. Another leather belt wrapped itself around his chest. He could barely budge. He was trapped.

At the desk, Mallory was busily tapping buttons and pulling levers. Jan had not even noticed them before.

"You all ready?" Mallory shouted over to Whitlow.

"Ready," said Whitlow. "Let them go."

Mallory pulled another lever. Jan's chair suddenly began to vibrate. It shook and quivered, and it hummed.

Jan cried out.

He could feel something—electricity—racing through his veins like fire.

He glared at Mallory, watching him work. Then the man began to grow indistinct. Jan whirled his head and tried to find Whitlow. He couldn't see him at all. The chair hummed on. Now the whole room was growing dark, dim, distant.

Then it faded completely from view.

Then there was nothing but the emptiness.

And the silence.

Jan knew where he was: this was the timevoid, the place outside the window, the stream that carried a person through time. He knew what it was, but he couldn't help himself:

He screamed.

And didn't hear a sound.

He was lost. Yes, lost and alone. He tried to shut his eyes to ward off the emptiness but that only seemed to make it worse. The blackness surrounded him everywhere. It seemed to creep nearer and nearer, threatening to engulf and swallow him.

He threw open his eyes. It was no better. Again, he screamed and screamed and screamed.

Still, there was no sound in the absolute void of time.

CHAPTER SIX

Overheard, a lone cloud, white and fluffy, floated gently through an otherwise clear sky. As a sight, the cloud was not extraordinary, yet Jan followed its serene flight with unaccustomed intensity.

He did not turn his gaze aside until a sudden voice said, "Are you Jan Jeroux?"

Then he looked. A strange, very tall, very skinny man dressed in brown buckskin stood beside him. The man peered down at Jan, who lay upon the ground.

"Me?" said Jan.

"I don't see anyone else hereabouts."

"But—" Jan couldn't seem to tear his mind away from the white cloud in the blue sky. "But who are you?"

A sudden lanky arm shot out from the man's side and, clasping Jan firmly by the wrist, drew him forcefully to his feet. "I'm Horatio Nextor."

"Yes," Jan agreed, grasping the hand and shaking it.

"So welcome home." Horatio Nextor dropped suddenly down upon the high grass and indicated that Jan should join him there.

So Jan sat down.

Reaching into his buckskin shirt, Horatio produced a cob pipe and a pouch of tobacco. "Care to share a smoke? It's good for the nerves."

"No, I don't smoke." The grass underneath was wet and the moistness easily penetrated the seat of Jan's green trousers. From the angle of the sun, he guessed it must be only a few hours past dawn. He wondered

43

how long he had been here. There were tall trees and white mountains everywhere. "Who are you?" Jan abruptly asked.

"I thought I told you. I'm Horatio Nextor. If what you mean is what am I, then I'm you boss."

"You're the squad leader?"

"That's right."

"In the time corps."

"Right again."

Jan shook his head in honest dismay. "I'm sorry if I sound like I'm an idiot but it—the timevoid—I just didn't know where I was for a long time."

"Well, I can tell you that. This place is in the Rocky mountains of the state of Wyoming in the year 1729, except it ain't really a state yet or even a full-fledged country."

"Wyoming . . . 1729 . . . yes, I think I remember now. Whitlow told us all about it."

"You don't have to feel bad. The technical people call it temporal disorientation. It hits most people on their first voyage through the stream."

"The others. Yes, I almost forgot about them. How is Gail? And—and—"

"Arthur Dodge. They're both doing fine. Arrived smack on target. I'm afraid you missed us by a day and a half-mile. Those idiots at the Academy are always doing that. In fifty-odd years in the corps, I've never missed a target by one hour or one yard." Horatio stood up. Jan noticed that he was holding a green valise in one hand and a long black object in the other.

"Is that gun?" Jan asked, standing also.

"A musket— yes."

"What do you use it for?" He was trying to recall the history of this period. "Indians?"

Horatio laughed. "Usually for food. The most Indians I've ever seen at one time hereabouts was the occasion when a good-sized band happened to stumble upon my cabin while I was out serving in time. Well,

44

it was a particularly lengthy voyage, so during my absence the band set up regular housekeeping on my doorstep. When I finally appeared among them, it set up a terrible discussion. Half were for killing me and the rest said I should be a god. I gathered they had never seen a white man before and, if some stories had reached them, they had chosen to dismiss it as so much balderdash. Well, I wasn't eager to be either dead or a god, so I invited them up to the cave where I keep my equipment. The chief and a few of his top warriors came in with me. I set the time traveling dials for two years ahead, disappeared, reappeared smack in the middle of them, and scared them clear out of the country. When I came back, of course they weren't there."

Horatio was leading Jan through a dense forest of tall evergreens. He had made no mention of where they might be going.

But Jan was patient and their destination was not long in coming. The path they had been following took a sudden twist and at the end of it was a wide open stretch of ground with a small log cabin seated directly in the middle of it.

"That's home," Horatio said.

"Is Gail there?"

"Her and the man both. I knew they'll both be overglad to see you. We've all been worried since you failed to show."

Jan was skeptical of Gail's eagerness, yet when they entered the drafty interior of the cabin, she leaped up from her seat beside a low table and welcomed Jan with surprising vigor.

He accepted the offer of her hand and shook it unhesitantly.

"I didn't know you cared," Jan said.

"Better the fool you know than one you don't," Gail said, smiling.

"Or vice versa," Horatio said, from where he was listening.

Arthur Dodge, who was also present, greeted Jan politely if not warmly. He seemed distracted, as if something were bothering him. Once the welcoming ceremonies were over, Arthur complained to Horatio that Gail had not allowed him to build a fire while they were alone. "Can't we do it now? I'm freezing to death."

"Nope," Horatio said. Going over to the table, he shoved aside a pile of dishes and pans and sat on the edge. He still held on to his musket. "Might attract Indians. After dark, it's okay to have one."

"But just a small fire. Only a little smoke." Arthur seemed almost to be pleading.

"So you can attract a small Indian." Horatio laughed and waved at Gail. "You listen to what the lady here says—she knows what's what."

"Well—" Arthur seemed uncertain. "Well, if you say so, but—" He shrugged, turned away, hesitated, then continued on to the far corner, where he sat on the floor, hugging himself and allowing his teeth to click.

Jan asked Gail, in a deliberately soft tone, "Something wrong with Arthur?"

"Nothing that wasn't wrong before." She whispered, too. "He's too old for this."

"Well, he's hardly as old as him." Jan indicated Horatio.

Gail shrugged. "Years don't matter. Arthur thought serving in time would be sweet and glorious. After one day, he already knows better. So he's disillusioned."

Jan, glancing around the cabin, could easily see why. It was a long way from a sweet and glorious sight. The cabin seemed to contain only the one big room, though there was a large round cavity in the ceiling above the fireplace that might have led to an additional chamber above. The low table—formed from several split logs bound together with twine—and the wooden bench beside it were the only articles of furniture present. Two wide gaps in the front wall allowed the chilly mountain air to penetrate the cabin interior in great, whooshing gusts.

Arthur was right about one thing. It was freezing cold in here.

Horatio called Jan over. "The first thing for you to do," he said, "is strip off that silly green suit. They're cute but just not suitable for wearing in any real environment. The second thing is for you to get something to eat." He looked past Jan and tried to meet Gail's eyes.

"Not me," she said flatly.

He sighed, looked briefly at Arthur, then returned his gaze to Jan. "I bet you're a great cook," he said. "Homestead boy and all that."

"Well, I can cook some," Jan admitted, "but I'm really not— "

"Then you've got yourself a job."

"Now wait a minute," Gail said. "Jan, don't let him fool you. Horatio cooked dinner last night after I made a mess of it and the meal was delicious."

Horatio eyed Jan carefully. "I suppose you're not any better a cook than her?"

"I doubt it," Jan said. "Worse, I bet."

"I was hoping you wouldn't say that. My stomach, you see, is the one really sensitive portion of my anatomy. But I hate to cook. My last squad, three very sharp boys, one of them could cook like the devil. I guess he must've spoiled me. This time I called the Academy and told them they better send me a woman. I figured that way I couldn't miss getting a cook. Instead, look what they sent me."

"I burned his eggs and he can't forgive that," Gail explained.

"Burned my coffee, too. What she did to the chicken I don't have the heart to describe. But let's get back to the clothes situation."

As Jan removed his green uniform, Horatio prowled the room, dragging forth a good dozen cardboard boxes. He spilled the contents of several on to the floor. Each

47

contained a choice of garments that seemed almost unlimited. Every conceivable period of American history was covered and there was a large assortment of various sizes. Jan pawed through shirts and skirts, pants and pantaloons, bustles and corsets, gowns and bikinis, stovepipe hats and fedoras, fur coats and paper jackets.

He finally selected a pair of plain but warm blue denim jeans and a heavy green sweatshirt.

Gail smiled in mock appreciation. "Now you look like a real corpsmen," she said.

Even Jan grinned—but at least he felt comfortable.

When Horatio finished building and lighting the fire, he turned his back on the rising flames and squatted on the hearth. "Jan, Gail, Arthur," he called. "Come on over here and gather around. I think it's time to begin your education."

Jan, his belly filled with hot soup, joined the others on the floor in front of Horatio. Even Arthur, with the advent of the fire, seemed relaxed and in a mellow mood.

"First off," Horatio said, "I want you to tell me where you finished in your Academy class. Gail?"

"I was first," she said, without emphasis.

"Arthur?"

"Second."

"Jan?"

"I was—ah—thirty-eighth."

Gail giggled. "And how many graduated?" she prodded.

"Thirty-eight," Jan admitted shamefully.

But Horatio appeared to pay no attention. "The reason I asked," he said, "is so that we would have all that out in the open and over and done with. If I hear any other comment about class standing or anything of that sort as long as you're here serving under me, it'll mean a certain demerit and a smack of extra duty. Now I said I was going to begin your education and that's exactly what I meant: begin. So you sit here and stay calm while I go and fetch my working tools."

He moved across the room till he stood underneath the round hole in the ceiling, then leaped up, stuck his hand through the opening, and pulled down a rope ladder. He ascended quickly and disappeared inside the gap.

"What did he mean?" Arthur asked. "Begin our education?"

"Got me," Gail said.

When Horatio returned, he was carrying a pair of matching fat books, one under each arm. He sat them down upon the hearth, then mounted the ladder again. He came down with two more similar volumes, then made a third trip. A fourth. A fifth. And a sixth.

By the time he was finished, he had an even dozen matching volumes piled in front of his feet.

"Now," he said, lifting the top book in his hands, "the reason I went and got these was to prove a particular point to you. Notice the title?" He turned the spine so that they could read. It said: *A Concise History of the United States of America, Volume VIII, 1945-1972.*

"That was our basic text at the Academy," Gail said.

"Text for what?"

"Why, American history, what else?"

"Well, you see, that was then and this is now. My job isn't American history so much as it is to teach you how to serve safely and intelligently in time. How long that'll take I have no idea, but nobody will leave this cabin until the task is done."

"I'm ready right now," Gail said.

"What makes you so sure?"

"There isn't a word in any of those books I don't already know. If you don't believe me, ask me."

Horatio grinned. "There's no need for that. I'd rather show you." Wheeling suddenly, he took the book he held and hurled it straight into the fire. Horrified,

Arthur sprang up as if to rescue the volume, but Horatio waved him sharply down. "Let it burn," he ordered.

And so it did.

Then, while the ashes floated up the chimney, Horatio took the next book in the stack and threw that into the flames. Then another and another and another until all twelve were burning.

Finally, he spoke. "There's no need to worry. That was just a little lesson and I've got a bunch more copies of the set upstairs. The point I was trying to make is simple: books don't teach, they educate. All three of you are, I'm sure, rightly and properly educated. But you haven't been taught and that's what I've got to do now."

"What sort of learning do you have in mind?" Arthur asked. There was more than a hint of hostility in his tone and Jan recalled that Arthur had been a teacher and historian.

"Oh, this type," Horatio said, and with lightning speed he reached out, caught Arthur by the arm, lifted him off the floor, and tossed him neatly and firmly across the room.

Arthur lay on his back, groaning, but he did not seem hurt.

Horatio leaned back and folded his hands in his lap. "What I'm going to teach you," he said, "is how much more there is to the past besides simple history."

Jan couldn't help smiling. He leaned across to Gail and whispered, "See? That's what I told you all along."

"Shut up," she told him. But her heart no longer seemed in it. She was watching poor Arthur struggling to regain his feet.

CHAPTER SEVEN

It took two full months for them to learn, heart and head, and during the interim they ate well, slaved vigorously, worked furiously, studied violently, and slept soundly.

When this second and more arduous training period was at last over, Horatio informed them by simply stating, after a typically long day of wrestling, tree-falling, scouting, and cabin building, "Why, you're not half-bad. I'm really amazed. I think you may just do. Tomorrow, we'll wander up to the cave and find out."

Jan gaped. The cave was the mysterious place where Horatio kept the time traveling equipment concealed. A dozen times in the past two months, he had deserted his squad for periods ranging up to four days in order to accomplish assigned missions and each time he had returned to find chaos awaiting him. But the most recent time, the chaos had been much less severe than before and Horatio had been visibly pleased. "Why, if that grizzly hadn't chased poor Arthur through my vegetable garden, this place might almost be livable."

But now that the actual announcement of their success had been made, none of them seemed willing to believe that it would really all be over.

Gail said, "But you can't mean that—"

"I mean you graduated," Horatio said. "Completed your course of training. I'm afraid I haven't any diplomas to hand out, so you'll just have to accept my word."

"Then we'll actually be voyaging upstream?" Arthur said.

51

"This morning I went down to the cave. There was a message from the Captain laying out an assignment. I read it and I figured, why should I be doing all this dirty junk alone? I've got three good corpsmen right here with me and I'm wasting them. So we'll all be going in the morning."

"But where?" Gail said. "When?"

Horatio grinned and shook his head. "Oh, somewhere," he said. "Sometime. Just make sure you catch a good night's sleep tonight. Tomorrow you're all going to be very busy."

If the others slept well that night, they did far better than Jan. If his eyes dropped shut for longer than a brief few seconds in time, it was news to him. The fact was that, come tomorrow morning, he would be voyaging into time, leaving this historical but uninhabited wilderness and venturing forth into the real past, where real flesh-and-blood people lived and breathed and worked.

He was excited by the prospect. But he was not afraid. While he still often missed the comforting past of the Jarman Homestead—sometimes homesickness affected him like a physical pain—he was also intrigued by this new life chosen for him, thrilled by its myriad possibilities. If he had hated the tedium of the Academy, he had come to love it here with Horatio, and he could not help wondering, as the night drained away, what would tomorrow bring?

Where would he be voyaging? And when?

He tried to imagine himself in various historical locales.

What about on the wide and wild frontier? A member of a band of bold pioneers, blazing a trail through the wilderness on the way to distant Oregon? Could that be it?

Or an observer of the great and terrible Southern Civil War of the 1850's, when four million slaves had risen in righteous and bloody anger at the inhuman treatment they had so long been forced to endure? Would he be able to bear such an event? Violence and war were significant aspects of the American past. In time, if he wished to serve the corps, he would have to learn to deal with such things. But was he ready yet for that?

But what about as a simple colonial artisan? Or a miner in search of gold in the Black Hills of Dakota? Or a member of the complex urban American of the late twentieth century?

There were so many possibilities. That was the problem. It seemed incredible to him how dramatically and drastically life had changed during the time—a mere four hundred years—in which he would be serving. And his visions of that uncertain world were never wholly complete. Too many gaping holes permeated his knowledge. This first voyage would most likely be little more than a sightseeing expedition. He didn't think Horatio would yet be willing to carry them into any of the more violent periods of the American past.

Still, he could dream, couldn't he?

What if he were a great multi-millionaire of the nineteenth century who, after amassing a fortune too gigantic to count, chose to give it all away to those many who truly needed it? An army of the poor would mob his great Park Avenue residence and he, their patron saint, seated behind a desk piled him with bags of gold, handing one to each as he approached and saying—

A hand rattled his shoulder.

Jan came awake. A slender toothpick shadow loomed over him. "Let's get moving," said the shadow.

"Horatio?"

"I've been called that."

"I—I—" Jan shook his head. "I think I was dreaming."

"No harm in that. Get up, get dressed, get down to the cave. After that, you can do all the dreaming you wish."

Arthur and Gail were already awake and dressed. Jan

joined them as soon as he could. When he did, Horatio threw him a pair of rough homespun trousers and a matching shirt. Horatio himself was dressed in a similar fashion, but both Gail and Arthur were decked out in rich and splendid outfits.

"But we're not going to different times, are we?" Jan asked, very much surprised.

"Who told you that?" Horatio said.

"Why, nobody said, but they're dressed—well, they're different."

"Of course they are. Don't you think Arthur would look rather silly in the gown?"

Horatio refused to explain any further.

When everyone was dressed, Horatio nodded toward the door. "Shall we go, then?"

Nobody said no, so out they went.

The sun had barely entered the morning sky and a heavy mist lay upon the grass. Horatio led them to the rear of the cabin and then plunged straight into the dense thicket of the forest. Gail followed, stepping with particular caution because of her wide gown, and Jan and Arthur brought up the rear. Nobody spoke a single word. Horatio seemed to know exactly where he was going even though Jan failed to make out any signs that might have marked a trail.

Soon enough, the trees fell away and they moved up a steep, rocky hillside. They had nearly reached the summit, when Horatio suddenly stopped beside a large scrub bush. "This is it," he said, as he grabbed the bush and lifted it easily off the ground. Underneath was a large, dark hole.

The cave, Jan thought.

Horatio pulled a flashlight out of his pocket and flicked it on. "I'll go in first and light the lantern. Gail, you come next. Jan, you and Arthur can fight over who gets the rear. Just remember to put the bush back in place when you do. We don't want anyone stumbling on this place by accident."

Jan nodded. He volunteered to enter the cave last.

After he had done so and replaced the scrub bush as directed, he turned and surveyed the cave. It was large and deep and dark. A bright lantern dangling from one wall succeeded in illuminating a small semi-circle of space. Within this area Horatio, Gail, and Arthur stood. Also located within the light was the time machine itself.

As far as Jan could tell, the device was the same as the one that had brought him here from the Academy. There were two large chairs sitting on the floor of the cave and a wide instrument panel that contained a variety of dials and levers. Horatio stood here, adjusting the dials. But there were other components as well that he had either failed to notice before or which had been hidden. The most puzzling of these was a large, transparent vat of pink liquid resting on stilts a good yard off the floor. Floating on the surface of this liquid were a pair of matching round balls. From the dark rear reaches of the cave, a generator could be heard loudly humming.

Horatio moved away from the instrument panel and indicated the others should join him. "I'm going to make this quick," he said, "because the first two of us are now set to leave here in three minutes. Gail, that will be you and Arthur. Jan and I will follow a few minutes later. We are all going to the same time and the same general place, New York City in November of 1840. We will remain there for exactly forty-eight hours, at which time we will be returned here to this cave whether you want to be or not. Arthur, you have voyaged through the stream before. Gail, you know plenty about it secondhand. I'll expect both of you to know how to handle yourselves. You're to establish residence at the best hotel you can find and, in the time you've got, live the best life you can imagine. Just stay out of trouble and use your heads for something more than balancing hats. Here—" he reached into a pocket and drew out a small leather pouch "—this is three hundred dollars in gold." He handed the pouch to Arthur. "It should serve you sufficiently. Now—any questions?"

"Yes," said Jan. "What about me?"

"You and I will be voyaging together. Same time, same city, different social sphere. Gail and Arthur, get in your chairs. You haven't much time."

Obediently, the two of them hurried over and strapped themselves down. It seemed to Jan that the generator began to hum even more loudly than before. He glanced over at the vat of pink liquid and saw that the floating balls were bouncing wildly up and down as though rocked by a savage wind.

When Jan looked back at the chairs, Gail and Arthur were no longer there—the chairs were empty.

"Wow," was all Jan could manage to say.

Horatio laughed. "I still say that, even after fifty years." He hurried over to the instrument panel, turned a couple dials, then went and sat down in one of the leather chairs. Jan joined him and took the opposite chair. Both strapped themselves in place.

Jan wanted to talk, say anything, discuss anything, but no subject seemed properly relevant. Several times he opened his mouth to speak but always chose, at the last moment, to choke back the words.

He was excited, yes, but he was also—he admitted this—frightened. Remembering the dreadful emptiness of the timevoid, he wondered if he was prepared to endure that infinite blackness again.

He was about to tell Horatio that he couldn't go through with it when his chair began to vibrate. He looked over at the vat and saw the balls bouncing wildly. He started to scream but hastily checked that urge. He would not cry out—the others hadn't—he would be brave, too. As horrible as it was, the timevoid did not extend indefinitely. He told himself this, silently, again and again.

Then, suddenly, there was nothing around him.

And he did scream.

But nothing came out.

Then he knew he was on his way and, abruptly, without logical reason, relaxed and shut his eyes and allowed the stream of time to sweep him effortlessly and inexorably forward.

CHAPTER EIGHT

In 1840, New York town—it could hardly be called a city in comparison to what was to come later—seemed to consist of nothing but one long and glorious party.

At least this was true of those portions of the town Horatio Nextor chose to reveal to Jan.

Within an hour of their arrival, Jan discovered first-hand that the native liquor was capable of burning the tender lining of his throat like a virulent form of acid and thereafter he swore off any alcohol and restricted his drinking to only enough water to prevent his mouth from going dry in the noxious tavern air they were constantly inhaling. Horatio, on the other hand, continued voluntarily to swill jug after jug of whiskey, brandy, gin and cider without displaying the least effect, either outwardly or within.

He told Jan, "I'd never be such a fool as to claim drink as the best manner in which to make a friend. It isn't—but it is the quickest. And, for our present limited purposes, speed is of the essence and the fact that the people we now meet may later, when sober, turn out to be entirely different creatures from those we have known isn't so important."

They stood trapped in the middle of a swirling mob. This particular tavern was typical of all they had visited: cold, bare, and smelling terribly of sawdust and spilled drink. A tinkling piano in some concealed corner filled the room with stale music hall ditties. They had been here an hour and not yet reached the bar. A bearded man in buckskin danced furiously past them, nearly knocking Jan to the floor, then bounced to the top of a table, where he continued his wild romp, shaking and twisting vaguely in rhythm to the rattling piano.

Jan held his ears and winced, but Horatio wore an intense grin of pleasure that never left his lips.

"Hey—hold on there." Horatio grabbed a tall, thin man in a clean black suit who was moving past them. "Don't I know you?"

The man turned and looked Horatio up and down. "You may. But I don't know you."

"Have you seen Sam?" Horatio asked.

The man nodded carefully and put out his hand. Horatio gripped it in an odd fashion and the two men shook.

"You a New York man?" he asked Horatio.

"Do I look it?" Horatio indicated his shabby appearance. Most of the other occupants of the tavern were dressed even more casually.

"Then where?"

"Kentucky."

The man nodded, "I'm not familiar with the brotherhood there."

"We're powerful. I just came North from Virginia myself."

"A fine state. Jefferson. A pity his descendants have turned so foul."

"More the descendants of Burr than Jefferson."

"Or the Pope. Here—" the man's hand appeared again and was shaken in the same odd manner "—I'm William Waite."

"Horatio Nextor. And this is Jan Jeroux."

William Waite's brows rose quizzically. "A Frenchman?"

"Only a distant grandparent," Horatio explained. "Native Americans for three generations back. I can testify to that myself."

"Relative of yours?"

"Cousin."

Waite nodded and shook Jan's hand but in the normal way. "Have you seen Sam?" he asked.

60

Jan shook his head, too confused to risk answering.

"Not yet," Horatio put in, "but when we reach home I'll see that he does."

"And the sooner you leave this godless town the better for him," Waite said.

"I understand it's this depression," Horatio said. "They tell me New York was a decent town before then. Our political victories in '37, for example."

"It's not the depression," Waite said. "It's the godless Irish who are back of it."

"Then how about sharing a drink with me?" Horatio suggested, waving in the general direction of the hidden bar.

"I'll purchase a quantity. Why don't you wait here and we'll step outside? I'm afraid that taverns do not agree with me. I came here only to meet a man."

"And did you?"

Waite eyed Horatio with clear suspicion and his reply, when it came, was terse: "He was delayed apparently."

"A pity—but at least we were able to meet."

"Exactly," said Waite. "Stay here and I'll be right back." He moved off into the crowd, muttering inaudibly to himself. Immediately, he was swallowed from view.

"Let's head for the door," Horatio said, as soon as Waite was gone. "I don't want him trying to sneak away without us."

"Why? Who is he?" Jan struggled to keep pace with Horatio, who was bulling a wide path through the crowd.

"Our assignment," Horatio said over his shoulder.

They popped on through the open doorway and stood at the edge of the dirt street. Jan was stunned to discover the sun shining brightly in the sky. Inside the tavern it had seemed like the middle of night while actually the hour was barely past four.

The street was hardly less crowded than the tavern. The inclusion of a variety of animals—most were horses but also a few cows—added to the general clamor. There seemed to be packs of roving, screaming children everywhere. A few had even penetrated the interior of the tavern. As Jan stood, a pair of urchins darted suddenly between his legs, nearly spilling him to the ground.

"Irish," Horatio said. "If Waite saw them, he'd froth at the mouth."

"But who is he? I mean, what is he? What did that handshake mean and who is Sam?"

"It's all mixed up with a thing called the Order of the Star-Spangled Banner, but—hush up—here he comes now."

Horatio stepped into the path of William Waite, who had just exited from the tavern, and stopped him from passing. Waite frowned at this sudden apparition.

"I see you got our bottle," Horatio said, pointing to a pint flask of gin in Waite's hand.

"Ah, yes. Care to share a swallow?"

"Gladly." Horatio accepted the bottle and took a deep swallow. He handed the flask back to Waite and said, "This is quite a day today, isn't it? I haven't seen so many people in one place since the time my maiden great-aunt got married at seventy-five. There's something about an election that seems to bring out the worst in men. Or maybe it's the best. I know it seems to cause them to drink a lot."

"It seems to affect you that way at least," said Waite.

"Oh, I always drink a lot." And, to prove his point, Horatio took another hefty swallow from the flask.

"Have you two cast your ballots yet?"

"No," Horatio said. "As I believe I mentioned, I am a citizen of another state. And Kentucky voted two weeks ago."

"And you missed that, too?"

"I was in Virginia at the time."

Waite rubbed his chin musingly. "Perhaps we can remedy that. I assume you're a Whig."

"Tippecanoe all the way," Horatio confirmed. "He swept Kentucky."

"But New York is all important. And Mr. Van Ruin's home."

"It will be soon. At the moment, he still has a house in Washington."

"Then come along," Waite said. He turned suddenly down the street and hurried away.

"Where you going?" Horatio called after him.

"We're going to vote." Waite waved eagerly. "Come on—the both of you."

Horatio shrugged, grabbed Jan, and the two of them darted around a lolling cow.

"You're not really going to let him do it, are you?" Jan said, in a hushed tone.

"Do what?"

"Vote."

"Why not?"

"Well, you're not a citizen of this time. Won't that change history and cause everything to—?"

Horatio chuckled sharply and patted Jan's arm. "You let me worry about that. If I get a chance, I'll explain later. But—come on—we better hurry. That fellow walks faster than a cat."

Horatio darted ahead to catch up with Waite but Jan, when he tried to follow, bumped into a stray child and sent the boy sprawling to the ground. By the time he had helped the child back to his feet and calmed the worst of his angry cries, Horatio and Waite were nearly out of sight far down the street.

Hollering, Jan hastened in pursuit but had to detour around a stumbling drunk, a squealing pig, and a half-dozen additional children.

The basic reason behind all of this—at least the drinking and the noise—was what Waite had mentioned: today was election day in New York State. The electors for the President of the United States would be chosen by a mass vote of all free, white, adult male citizens. The contest was being waged between the current President, Martin Van Buren, a native of New York and leader of the Democratic forces of Tammany Hall, and

William Henry Harrison, an aging hero of an obscure Indian war who represented the opposition Whig party. Horatio had refused to tell Jan who won and, if he had ever known, the fact escaped him now.

But, if the outcome truly mattered in the least, nothing here had shown him any evidence of that. Every man seemed violently in favor of one candidate or the other but nobody seemed quite able to explain why.

Still, these celebrations were mighty events to behold.

And, once night fell, it would get even wilder. Horatio said, "Wait'll you see their torchlight victory parades. Not one, mind you, but two, for nobody can be certain of the actual victor for days to come and who wants to concede defeat when they can just as easily claim a win?"

When Jan finally succeeded in catching up to Horatio and Waite, he thereafter stuck close to their heels. Waite, speaking only when necessary, led them through a confusing series of narrow and often filthy alleyways. As much as anything else in this time, the presence of so much raw garbage and sewage in the open streets had taken a deal of getting used to. Jan had to hold his breath and grab his stomach when passing through some of the worst areas. Both Horatio and Waite seemed oddly immune to the reeking odors.

They ended up at last along the waterfront. There were no celebrants down here, only a few sailors and dockworkers. The sight of the high sailing ships, their giant masts rising like geometric clouds against the distant dying sky, was one of the most impressive things Jan had seen in this time.

Waite stopped them suddenly and turned to caution: "This here has got to be secret now. We don't want a word of it leaking out. Tammany will cheat like the devil himself but she don't like to have the tables turned in her face. Understand?"

"Mum's the word," Horatio said.

"And you, son? You intending to do your part?"

"I don't think I'm old enough," Jan said.

Waite chuckled. "That can't matter, can it? When you're casting a phoney vote, it don't matter if it's two times phoney or only one. I'd vote a slave if I thought I could get away with it."

For some reason, this struck Jan as very wrong. "But what's the purpose," he asked, "of holding a free election if you're going to cheat?"

Waite answered heatedly: "Because of them. Don't you think they're cheating, too, only worse. It all goes back to their blackguard President, Colonel Burr. He cheated himself into the White House twice, so Andy Jackson thought he could do the same. Now his deceitful heir, Sweet Sandy Whiskers, has done likewise. We ain't going to allow it to happen another time. This is war, son, a sacred struggle for self-preservation which makes it a deeper conflict than any with the French or the English. And when I speak of that, I ain't referring to the preservation of myself or yourself or hisself or even of Colonel Harrison's self but rather of this whole gorgeous country, the native American land."

"But don't the Democrats live here, too?"

"Some do, that is true." Waite visibly calmed himself but soon grew excited again. "But others are different. There are certain blasphemous, ungodly forces set loose from the rotting bosom of Mother Europe who now wish to run havoc through our once purified streets. No, sir. Unchained and uncontested, they will tear this land asunder. America will become but a prisoner, a vassal of Italy. If we want to win this holy war, we've got to stick together. Every native American has to do his part. Ain't that right, Mr. Nextor?"

"I couldn't have put it any better myself." Horatio nodded thoughtfully. "Jan, if you wish to vote, then do so."

"Then I guess I will," he said. But only because he thought that's what Horatio wanted.

Waite slapped him soundly on the back. "Good lad." He quickly became conspiratorial. "Now—both of you

—I want you to stay right here while I reconnoiter the area and make sure the operation is running smoothly." He pressed a finger to his lips. "And if anyone comes by asking loose questions, you know nothing. You're country boys watching the big ships and that's it. You never heard of any William Waite. Remember that?"

"Of course," Horatio said.

Waite nodded hastily, then backed around a wooden shed and disappeared from view.

"What was he talking about?" Jan asked Horatio when they were alone. "When he was raving to me?"

"Oh, the Irish, I guess. It's hard to say. A fair number of Americans of this era were frightened for reasons I have never quite been able to fathom by the rising tide of immigrants coming here from Europe. It isn't that the country ever belonged to them. Most seem to have forgotten that their own ancestors had all come here by boat at one time or another. It's generally called the native American movement, which I find rather amusing, given the true facts. The only native Americans I know are Indians. If you asked Waite about them, he'd call them savages. At least—unlike Waite and his ilk—they were not bigots."

"Then you knew about Waite before we came here?"

"I told you he was our assignment. We've got to study his actions and those of his followers during this election."

"You didn't tell me that before."

"There wasn't any need. I wanted you to enjoy the time for what it was worth. I still want you to do that. These are good times even taking into consideration men like William Waite and other—" Horatio nodded toward a pair of men walking past, one white and one black "—similar aberrations."

Jan watched the master and his slave until the two of them had passed out of sight. He felt powerfully and deeply depressed and it was a time before he could speak. Here in free New York the existence of slavery in much of the rest of the country had been a hidden

66

fact. Now that he was reminded of it, he found it difficult to forget again.

"Where did he go?" he asked, at last.

"Oh, probably to check on us. You remember he didn't like me asking about his secret meeting. He'll undoubtedly check to see we're not spies for Tammany."

"Then you are going to go and vote?"

"Sure. It's the only way to prove my loyalty to him. The handshake isn't enough for a suspicious fellow like Waite."

"But won't that create a paradox? I mean, you're not really a person in this time."

Horatio smiled. "Paradoxes are a good deal harder to create than that. Time—history—it's like a big river. It's not easy to dam those powerful waters. If I vote, it won't stay. The waters will sweep it easily away."

"Then your vote won't count."

"Nope. No more than we will. If we went home right now, hopped back into the chair, voyaged back to this same time and spot, know what we'd find? An empty chunk of space. That's what."

"I see. I think."

"Then let me tell you a story. A true story, too, and maybe it'll help make things come more clearly. Once upon a time, there was a time corpsman—let's call him Horace—who violated the most basic precept of them all: he fell in love with a lady from the stream. The year in which this occurred was not, strangely, terribly far distant from this time, and the place, strangely again, was right here in America. The lady, whose name was Ann Rutledge, struck poor Horace as the most beautiful, kind, strong, loving human being he had ever met. Unfortunately for him, this love turned out to be a one-sided affair, for Ann preferred a young man of her own time whose name was Abe Lincoln. Well, it eventually came to pass that Ann fell ill. Knowing his history, Horace was already aware that she was fated to die. He couldn't stand it—he just couldn't let it happen. So

67

what he did—and it was no easy process, I assure you—was sneak into the Academy office and steal a few vials of one of our modern wonder drugs. He then returned downstream and he saved Ann Rutledge's life. It didn't mean she loved him even then. She did not. She loved Lincoln. But the sight of her alive again was enough to make Horace feel that he had done right."

Horatio paused, as if he were considering some insurmountable problem or else, perhaps, simply remembering something from long ago.

Finally, unwilling to bear the wait, Jan said, "But what's the point?"

Horatio blinked and shook his head. "Oh, I forgot to tell you that, didn't I? Well, the point is that Horace hadn't succeeded—he had, in fact, failed and failed miserably. A week passed. Maybe even two. It's hard to say. During this time, Ann Rutledge walked and lived and laughed and breathed. And then—*poof*—the dream was over. Ann was gone and not only was she dead but she had never even survived to live. Her body lay in the cold ground and when poor Horace went to visit the gravesite the granite marker told him she had died on the very day when he thought he had saved her.

"Needless to say, the Captain summoned Horace to the Academy and delivered a severe reprimand. He not only told Horace straight out what a fool he was but also explained what a bigger fool he would have been had he succeeded. Lincoln, as you must have guessed, was the real subject of that particular voyage. In the 1860's, following the great slave uprising in the South, he became President of the United States and helped to bind up the nation's many wounds. Had Ann Rutledge survived her illness, she and Lincoln would have been married and a happily married Lincoln would have sacrificed his later ambitions for simple contentment and never reached for his country's highest office. In other words, if poor dumb Horace had had his way, the entire fabric of American history might have been altered for the worse. But time was too strong for that.

It resisted Horace and beat him down. Ann Rutledge died. As she should have—and must have:"

"Then there's no way to change time?" Jan said. "We don't even have to worry about it."

"You're half right. Don't worry—it won't happen by accident."

"But there is a way?"

Horatio nodded. "Could be. Why don't you think on it and see if you can come up with an answer. I'm willing to bet you've got more brains in an earlobe than old Horace had in his entire head."

"But aren't you—?"

"Hush up. Here he comes now."

True enough, William Waite had appeared around the corner of the shed and was fast approaching them. When he arrived, he said, "All set— no problems."

"Then you decided we weren't Tammany spics," said Horatio.

"Why, the thought never entered my mind that you were."

Waite then led Jan and Horatio down the waterfront until they reached a large stone building. A small sign beside the door identified the structure as a subsidiary customs house. The officer-in-charge flashed a wide grin when Jan and Horatio entered the spacious lobby. Without a word, he handed them both long paper ballots inscribed with a variety of names.

Leaning past Horatio's shoulder, Waite helpfully tapped one column of names: "Those are our electors."

"The Whigs?"

"Right."

With a pen borrowed from the customs officer, Horatio swiftly marked his ballot with broad dark X's. Jan did likewise, though not without some hesitation. The past, it seemed to him, should be treated with more reverence than this; it shouldn't be tampered with for no powerfully good reason.

"Hurry up," Waite prodded, when he saw Jan pause. "We haven't got the day and night, boy."

Jan nodded tightly and finished marking his ballot. Waite clapped him on the shoulder and said:

"Now let's go get us a few drinks to celebrate."

Jan shrugged. "Okay."

Waite suddenly glared and removed his hand hastily from Jan's shoulder. "What was that you just said?"

"I said okay." Jan couldn't understand Waite's reaction.

"Okay what?" Waite glared more violently than ever before. The customs officer appeared very upset as well.

Horatio rushed in quickly to explain: "Jan only meant he'd be pleased to go with you. That expression has gained considerable popularity on the frontier. He meant no harm."

"Well, here in New York," Waite said, "when a man says O.K. he can be referring to only one thing and that is Old Kinderhook Van Buren himself."

"Jan meant nothing like that at all. Did you, Jan?"

"No, sir."

"Well, I still don't like it. It's not the kind of slip I like to hear."

"Aren't those ballots sufficient proof of our loyalty?" Horatio said.

Waite considered this. At last he nodded tightly. "I guess they are. Son, I apologize."

"That's all right," Jan murmured.

"Tom, I'll talk to you later." Waite nodded to the customs officer. "Let's go."

The three of them stepped outside. As they moved along the waterfront, retracing their steps, Waite explained about the customs officer: "A traitor to Tammany." It was growing dark now and they walked carefully. "When all our special ballots are properly marked, he'll carry them downtown and stuff them in a Tammany ballot box while they think he's working for them." Waite cackled with unrestrained glee. "When we win the election, that man'll have to be made a judge. He's just the kind we need."

70

Shortly before the polls were due to close, Waite left them suddenly, saying he had to go downtown and meet a man. Horatio offered to go with him, but Waite demurred politely and firmly.

As soon as Waite had hastened off down the street, Horatio signaled Jan that they were to follow.

By the time they turned the first corner, Waite had disappeared from view. He might have been plucked bodily from the street by a guardian angel.

Horatio swore softly.

"I'm sorry," Jan said. "I suppose this is my fault for saying okay."

Horatio shook his head and continued downtown. "I think you could have said anything you wanted and it wouldn't have mattered. William Waite is no fool. He's never apt to be called too trusting. He used us for the purposes he wished and now he wants to get out of the way."

"So what do we do now?"

"We keep walking. Until we decide to stop. Then we do stop."

They had entered a more densely populated section of the city now. People of all sorts—workingmen, merchants, farmers and ordinary ruffians—filled the streets. An atmosphere of anticipation hung over the crowd, as if some important event were about to occur. So many of them were holding and carrying torches that the light they cast was only slightly less bright than that of midday.

"But does this mean our assignment is over?" Jan asked.

"What assignment is that?"

"Waite. Now that we've lost him."

"Oh, we'll find him again."

"How can you be sure?" Jan waved at the huge crowd surrounding them. "It's like trying to find a beetle in a corn patch."

"But Waite's not a beetle. This may be a big town, Jan, but it's also a small world."

"What does that mean?"

Horatio grinned and winked. "You'll see."

Jan noticed that a wide strip of ground in the center of the roadway was being left unoccupied up and down the street. Horatio finally came to a stop at the edge of this open space.

"Is there some reason why we can't stand out there?" Jan asked.

"Because we're supposed to be waiting. The victory parades—both of them—are supposed to be passing here shortly."

Then they waited. Horatio had timed it well enough so that it wasn't more than ten minutes later when the Whig parade came into view. The size of this contingent was not huge but this lack was more than made up for by the amount of noise and enthusiasm generated by those present. Their signs and banners waved through the air—each proclaiming, boldly, "Tippecanoe and Tyler, too"—while two men passed out gallon jugs of hard cider from a horse cart. Jan tried to swallow from the bottle Horatio obtained but the staff tasted worse than pure vinegar. Horatio, meanwhile, retrieved the jug and drained it. Then he wandered briefly off in search of more.

This first group did not prove to be the end of the Whig celebration. They had barely disappeared down the street when a second contingent appeared, this one including a band. The only tune the musicians seemed to know was "Yankee Doodle" and Jan suffered through a dozen renditions in less than ten minutes. The final portion of the Whig parade consisted of a half-size log cabin being lugged down the street upon the backs of a dozen sweating men.

Horatio hooted at the sight. "Harrison was no more born in a log cabin than you or me, Jan, but he sure managed to start a painful trend. Even into the middle twentieth century, politicians felt constrained to proclaim their humble—and often false—origins. President Huey Long in the late 1930's was the worst of the bunch—he finally reached the point where he was bragging of being born at the bottom of a bug-infested swamp. That's when the reaction finally set in and it so became that you had to be able to prove you had been born in a glass palace in the middle of Spain. Otherwise, you were always suspected of seeking high office in order to loot the public funds."

The Tammany Democrats came into view a few short moments folowing the passing of the log cabin. There were many more men in this group and their parade was wilder, less organized, brasher, more drunken, and far less given to silent tolerance in the face of noisy opposition jibes. The Democrats brought with them not one band but two, although both refused to play a thing beyond "Yankee Doodle." Jan held his ears at the end. A brief rumor rushed through the crowd that O.K. Van Buren himself would soon be appearing. Oddly, no spark was lit by this announcement. A man standing near to Jan spoke longingly of rushing home to fetch a hanging rope. In any event, Van Buren never came.

When the parade had passed, Horatio admitted his disappointment that Van Buren had not attempted to duplicate Harrison's phoney cabin. "Why, Matty Van was born in the upstairs room of his father's tavern. Just think of that, Jan—what a glorious sight to behold—a miniature two-story tavern being hauled through the streets of New York on the tired backs of a bunch of drunks."

"The Whigs weren't drunk."

"That's why I voted for Matty."

"But you didn't. Waite had you——"

"Tut, Jan, you underestimate me." Horatio dug into his pockets and came up with a pair of paper ballots. One Jan recognized as the vote he had cast earlier in the day. "For these I substituted a couple marked more to my liking. I'm afraid that customs officer isn't quite ready for that judgeship."

"But how did you ever do it?"

"Sleight of the hand, Jan, sleight of the hand."

All the while they had been watching the parades, Horatio had been keeping at least one eye peeled on the crowd itself. He was clearly looking for someone and Jan assumed it must be Waite. He tried to look, too.

Then, just as the last few Tammany stragglers were passing and Horatio was shoving the purloined ballots back into his pocket, he gave an abrupt grunt. "Be right back, Jan." And he moved hastily away into the crowd.

Jan started to go after him.

Horatio moved quickly, like a man with a purpose, but he had not gone far when he suddenly lurched to one side and rammed his shoulder into the unsuspecting spine of a man Jan had never seen before. The stranger was small, fragile, and pale, with long yellow hair. He was dressed in a plush frilly outfit, more evocative of Paris than New York. A pair of black slaves walked behind him.

The man struggled to recover his balance after Horatio's first onslaught and had nearly succeeded in doing so when Horatio bumped him again. This time there was no hope. The man tumbled completely over and landed in a horse trough.

Horatio jumped back as the water splashed.

One of the slaves grabbed at him but Horatio pushed him gently back. "Leave off, friend. An accident."

The slave, clearly startled by the familiar form of address, stepped away from Horatio.

When the little dandy emerged from his bath, he was coughing and sputtering, either from simple fright or pure rage. His voice, when he spoke, was so deeply Southern as to be almost undecipherable:

"You incredible, base, idiotic, sloven, savage, loathsome pig. How—how dare you attack me that way?"

He appeared to be addressing Horatio, who scratched his chin cautiously. "An accident, friend."

"And you two fools," the man said, turning to his slaves. "What are you doing? Laughing at me? Get over here at once." As he tried to extract himself from the trough, he kept sliding back in, dunking his head each time. Finally, with the languid assistance of the slaves, he reached dry land.

Horatio lit his pipe in apparent serenity.

The little man shook an enraged fist. He repeated his previous charges against Horatio and added several more he had apparently neglected to include.

Horatio repeated, "An accident, friend."

A small but amused crowd had gathered to watch. Jan noted that Horatio continued to survey the faces surrounding him.

"I must have satisfaction," the dandy was saying. "That is the only conceivable solution to this outrage. I really must demand it."

"Eh?" said Horatio, cupping an ear as if struck deaf. "What say, friend?"

A helpful by-stander shouted into Horatio's other ear: "Says he wants to fight a duel."

"Duel? Me?" Horatio shook his head dimly and waved both fists wildly in the air as if struggling with some invisible enemy. "It was a fair fight, I'm telling you. Ain't nobody can prove different. Sure, I shot him dead, but I'd been killing Indians thirty years before that and nobody said I should be hanged."

"No," the by-stander struggled to explain. "He don't care about that. He says he wants to fight you now."

"That's right." Horatio nodded expansively, banging his chin against his shirt front. "A fair fight. Killed my first man in eighteen hundred and zero-nine. Shot forty million Indians between the eyes. Hang their scalps from my belt."

"Then you accept his challenge?"

"I never minded another killing. Long as I get to wear the scalp." Horatio made a slicing motion with his hand through the air.

The by-stander turned to the dandy. "You've got yourself a duel, sir."

But the other man was already turning away. "Oh, bother that. I can't very well—"

"You scared?" said a voice out of the crowd.

The man was indignant. "That has nothing to do with it. I simply—simply refuse to fight—or kill—any man who isn't wholly competent. Yes, that's it. This fellow is clearly insane." He kept a close eye fixed on Horatio, as if fearful of setting off a sudden, mad attack.

But Horatio remained as he was, making slashing motions with his hands, cutting the air.

"I'll simply retire to my hotel and change clothes at once. There is really no need to prolong this affair."

"He's scared, all right," said another voice from the crowd. But the dandy was able to ignore this. Waving at his slaves, he stalked angrily and briskly down the street, leaving behind a dark puddle of spilled water.

"What was that all about?" Jan asked Horatio, once the crowd had dispersed.

"An accident. Guess I'm going to have to learn to watch where I'm going."

"But it looked to me as if you ran into him on purpose."

"Did it? Hey—look—there's our man." Horatio pointed across the street to where the now familiar figure of William Waite could be seen leaning against a storefront. His expression seemed bemused and puzzled. His eyes surveyed the passing crowd but he seemed to find no satisfaction there.

"Let's go see him," Horatio said.

When Waite spied Horatio and Jan approaching, he seemed less than pleased.

"What are you doing here?" he asked them, with open suspicion.

"Same thing as you, I suppose. Watching our victory parade."

"Oh, yes. Of course." His eyes never left the crowd. "I'm sorry for snapping at you but I'm upset. There was a fellow supposed to meet me here and I haven't seen a thing of him. You don't happen to know the time, do you?"

Horatio claimed he did: "It's past midnight."

"Oh, no. How could that be? I didn't guess it was

much past eleven and the man was supposed to meet me at ten-thirty. This was important—very important. The whole fate of our movement may have depended on this."

"Why don't you describe the fellow?" Horatio suggested helpfully. "Jan and I been around here some time and we may have bumped into him."

"He's a southerner. Plantation lad. Supposed to be kind of small, a snappy dresser, wears his hair long in the Southern fashion. It's blond, too. Actually, I've never met him myself, but we've corresponded to some degree. His father owns more than a thousand slaves. Biggest rice plantation in the whole country."

Horatio nodded firmly as if confirming a suspicion. "Jan, doesn't that sound like that character who caused all the commotion around here?"

"You mean the one you—?"

"Yeah, him." Horatio faced Waite. "Got himself arrested for being drunk. Tried to take a bath in a horse trough. Had a pair of slaves with him, too. Must be the same fellow."

"Oh, no. How could he do such a stupid thing?"

"Well, these elections bring out the worst in many men." Horatio shook his head philosophically. "But how about you and I grabbing a drink? It'll ease your mind, I imagine."

But Waite was clearly in no mood for drink. "This is terrible. I have to leave New York tomorrow night and I don't even know where the man is staying. We agreed to meet here and now I'll never be able to find him."

"You might ask a constable," Horatio said. "Now about that drink."

Distressed and distracted, Waite shook his head. He made a few apologies and then moved slowly away, his head hanging.

Jan asked, "Now what? Do we follow?"

"Nope," Horatio said. "I've had my fill of Mr. Waite and his ilk. I don't know about you but I'm going to go get me that drink."

"But won't he get away?"

"I suppose so. Let him."

"That person you bumped. Wasn't he—?"

Horatio laughed. "Wasn't that an incredible coincidence? Me having that accident and then Waite wanting to see him."

"But he wasn't arrested. He just went to change his clothes."

"I said that to protect Waite's health. He might get sick standing on a cold streetcorner this time of the year. Come on. Let's find that open tavern."

They suffered little difficulty finding such an establishment. Entering, Jan was amazed to discover that it was barely eleven o'clock.

"You told Waite it was past midnight."

"Did I?" Horatio said, driftly swiftly toward the bar. "I guess I erred again."

He ordered gin.

Jan's second day in 1840 proved much less eventful than the first. Awaking with a violent headache, Horatio refused to budge from bed till noon. By the time they reached the street, the news was fairly definite that Harrison had carried New York's electoral votes and with them the election.

Horatio laughed at the news and said, "There is always such a thing as an act of God. You can't ignore it."

"You mean Harrison really hasn't won?"

"I didn't say that."

They spent the remainder of that day and most of the night in touring the city, seeing the famous places but also examining more than a few of the more obscure nooks and corners. Horatio said he wanted Jan to have a chance to soak up the atmosphere of the time and place so that when he returned next it would seem as familiar to him as his own native land.

Once in the early evening, while wandering through a wealthy section of the city, Jan thought he recognized

Gail and Arthur crossing through a green square ahead of them.

He gave a shout and started to pursue but Horatio grabbed him firmly by the arm.

"Never do that, Jan, never. Back here none of us ever knows another. Don't ever forget that."

"Yes, sir. But was it really them?"

"I don't know. Or care. It's not my business or yours."

"Yes, sir."

"I mean that, Jan."

"I know you do, sir."

As midnight, the hour when the time machine would whisk them home, drew near, Jan and Horatio moved in the darker, less populated streets where they had first arrived. Horatio steered Jan into a dim tavern lightly occupied by a handful of battered old sailors. It was too late for eating or drinking; in less than an hour they would be swimming down the timestream.

"What do you think, Jan? Was the trip interesting enough for you? Do you feel you learned anything?"

"Yes, I believe I did. I hope it worked out the same for you, too."

"Huh? What do you mean?"

"About William Waite. We haven't seen him all day."

"Oh, that was taken care of," Horatio said flatly. "We don't need to worry about him any more." He glanced at his special timepiece. "We better go."

They moved into the street. Horatio pointed them down a dark alleyway. Crouching way down in the shadows where no random passer-by would be apt to observe them, they waited as patiently as they could.

"Nervous, Jan?"

"A little, I guess."

"Still afraid of the timestream?"

"Some, I guess."

"No need to be ashamed. Everybody's afraid at first. I've seen them scream and cry and beg me not to force them to go. You'll get over it. It takes time but sooner or later most people come to feel the way I do about it. That emptiness, that nothingness, it isn't frightening. What it is is serene. You get to feeling that this is how the universe must have been before the moment of that first big bang of creation. It's an awesome feeling but also strangely peaceful."

"I think I know what you mean."

"If you don't know, you will."

Jan heard a distant clock bonging out the hour.

A moment later, Horatio began to disappear.

When they arrived in the cave, Gail was there ahead of them. Her once pure white gown was stained and splattered in red. She was alone.

"What happened?" cried Horatio, struggling to free himself from the chair. "Where's Dodge?"

"Dead!" screamed Gail. "Shot! They blew his head right off and there was blood everywhere! They killed him—he's dead!"

CHAPTER NINE

Horatio took Gail softly in his arms and drew her close. Stroking her hair, patting her shoulders, he repeated that everything was going to be all right. At first, Gail appeared not to believe him. She continued to weep and wail. But, slowly, through cautious stages, she calmed down.

Finally, Horatio was able to push her gently away. "Let's go home," he said.

The three of them left the cave and passed into the dim light of early morning. Horatio held Gail's hand as they moved down the steep hillside and entered the thickness of the forest.

Jan, too stunned to utter a word, tagged behind. He could hardly believe what had happened. Arthur killed? But how? And why? And by whom?

At the cabin, Horatio seated Gail on the bench, then brought her a tall drink from his private stock of brandy. This seemed to calm her further. She wiped her nose, dried her eyes and, at Horatio's urging, managed a brief, fleeting smile.

Horatio then poured a second, bigger drink of brandy and had her swallow that. He sipped from the bottle himself. "Now," he said, dropping to the floor at her feet, "think you can tell me about it?"

"I have to? So soon?"

"It could be an emergency, Gail. I'm your squad leader and I've got to know."

"Yes, I suppose so."

"Then will you tell me?"

She did—haltingly at first—describing how she and

Arthur Dodge had spent two wonderful days within the prancing, high-fashion world of mid-nineteenth century New York. Nothing had gone wrong to spoil it. There had been some sort of commotion among the street rabble—Jan realized she was referring to the election—but otherwise nothing to interfere with the serene bliss of their nights and days. They had strolled the best streets, eaten in the finest restaurants, spoken only to the most respectable people, and slept in the best hotel in New York. As she spoke of these hours, she seemed able to forget the ugliness that was to come later.

Eventually, she came to their final day. She remembered suggesting a quiet walk as a fitting conclusion to the voyage. They had gone out that night. They walked through a pleasant square, met some people they had known, and finally ended up with a fine French dinner. By the time they left the restaurant, it was after eleven.

"We were just standing on the street, trying to decide what to do next when these two men came up and started talking to Arthur."

"What did they look like?" Horatio asked.

"Well, they had beards."

"Disguises?"

"I don't know—maybe."

"Well, what did they say?"

"I'm not sure about that, either. They spoke to Arthur, not to me, and they whispered. I just thought they were asking the time or directions, so I didn't try to overhear."

"Then what?"

"Then they drew out their guns and they shot Arthur. It was so sudden I never knew what was happening. It happened in a flash and then he was lying on the ground and the two men were running. I think I crouched down to see if I could help him—if he was dead—and that's when I got the blood on my gown."

"And he was dead?"

She faltered somewhat here: "Yes."

"And then?"

"Well, I think I must have screamed. A crowd gathered and a lot of men were asking me questions. One of them said he was a magistrate—a constable— whatever they were called. He said I had to come with him. I said I wouldn't. He said I had to. Then I got mad because the way he was acting it was like he thought I was the one who had killed poor Arthur."

"He probably did think so."

"Anyway, we argued. Then his voice started to get dimmer and dimmer. The next thing I knew he was gone and I was swimming through the timestream. Then I arrived here. I got out of the chair as fast as I could and then you and Jan came."

"That was a mistake," Horatio said.

She seemed shocked. "What was?"

"Disappearing in the middle of a crowd. You ought to know better than that."

"Well, I wasn't exactly watching the clock."

"Then you should have been. You're a corpsman, Gail, and that means you have to know how to think clearly and calmly. At all times. Under any circumstances."

She was sarcastic: "I'm really very sorry, Horatio. Next time somebody gets murdered in front of my eyes, I'll try to do better."

Horatio nodded. "That's all I ask, Gail."

"But who did it?" Jan had kept quiet until now but his natural curiosity refused to stay buried a second longer. "Do you know, Horatio?"

"I know it was two men with beards." He appeared distracted. Getting to his feet, he turned toward the door. "I'm going to drop a line to the Academy and tell them what happened. We'll need a replacement for Arthur. I'll return in an hour. Jan, take care of Gail until then."

"Yes, sir."

Then Horatio went out.

When he returned to the cabin—after exactly an

hour, as promised—the first thing Horatio did was wave at the boxes of clothes tucked in one corner. "Get dressed," he ordered. "Both of you." Dropping to the floor, he began pawing through the various garments, tossing a few out to Gail and Jan.

"But," said Jan, looking at the clothes, "you can't be sending us into the stream."

Horatio said nothing. He held up a bright blue-and-gold shirt that glowed in the dim light. "Jan, this'll be for you."

"Where are we going?" Gail asked. She was already dressing. Horatio had given her a silver skirt barely wider than a horsefly's wing and a pair of thigh-high glass boots.

"Middle of the twenty-first century. April 19, 2056, to be specific."

"What happened then?"

"Nothing. But I can't think of a safer, sweeter, nicer period in all of history. Or a duller one. Anyway, it'll give you chance to rest."

Jan thought this a good moment to renew his protest: "Isn't this kind of callous, Horatio? After all, Gail just had an ugly shock. Couldn't she rest here just as well?"

"I'm expecting you to do more than rest. I'll want a complete report on the time. This is an assignment, too. Don't forget that."

"But that's even worse. Gail can't—"

"Gail will, or I'll transfer her. The same goes for you, Jan. Anytime you don't like an order of mine, just say so. I'll see that your transfer is approved."

"But I don't want a transfer."

"Then your best bet is to keep your mouth shut or I'll get you one, whether you desire it or not." He pulled a bright orange bushy wig out of the box in front of him. "Here, Jan—this is for you."

Feeling like a total idiot, Jan placed the wig on top of his head. He didn't say a word.

"If I felt I needed you two here at the cabin," Horatio said, "I'd let you stay. But I don't need you. Since there's work to be done, I expect you to do it. Is that clear?"

"Yes, Horatio," said Jan and Gail, nearly in unison.

He stood up and waved at the door. "Then let's head for the cave. On the way I'll fill you in on the details to look for."

"What is our duration?" Gail asked, all business now.

"Four days."

For his part, Jan kept his big mouth tightly and firmly sealed.

CHAPTER TEN

Again, Jan floated through the absolute nothingness of the timevoid but this time the urge—or need—to scream and cry or shout no longer drove him. Instead, he thought it was peaceful here. The silence and darkness and emptiness calmed him. His eyes were shut and he watched soft dreams flowing gently past. He sighed. What was this place? This timevoid? It was a bridge— that was all—a passage between worlds, twin realities. He voyaged from 2056 to 1729, with nothing in between and therefore nothing to fear.

Suddenly, there was light. He opened his eyes. The cave again. Cold. He shivered. In the chair beside him, Gail sat.

Home again, home again.

"No trouble?" asked a familiar voice. Horatio's.

"No, everything went just—" Jan stopped. Across the room Horatio wasn't alone; beside him stood another man.

Jan sucked in his breath. The new man was Kirk Rayburn.

Arthur's replacement? He almost had to be.

Horatio came forward, drawing Kirk with him. "I believe you three know each other."

Gail seemed very pleased. Jan recalled how she and Kirk had always been friends at the Academy. He remembered how Kirk had played up to her and was suddenly swept by a flash of deep anger.

Gail held out her hand to Kirk. "Am I ever glad to see you here."

Kirk seemed no less overjoyed. "And so am I." He

grabbed her hand in both of his and squeezed warmly. "I've just had an awful time, Gail. You're the best thing that's happened to me in months."

"You heard about poor Arthur?"

"Yes, that was really terrible. Of course, it's also why I'm here." He finally decided to release her hand. "It must have been terrible for you."

"Oh, it was. Dreadful."

Jan smirked. The way she had been acting in 2056, he didn't think it could have been that dreadful.

"Later," said Kirk, "when we're alone, just the two of us, you'll have to tell me. It's the best way."

Jan couldn't remain silent any longer in the face of such monstrous phoniness. "Why don't we all get out of here?" he suggested. "Go home and—" he eyed Gail's blatantly exposed body "—and get decently dressed."

Kirk spun on him with an enormous smile. "And Jan Jeroux, too," he said. "I can hardly believe it." A hand snaked out from his side. "I can't say how glad I am."

Jan accepted the hand tepidly. "Then don't."

"Why, Jan and I were best friends at the Academy," Kirk told Horatio. "If it wasn't for the help I gave him, I bet he'd be floating in the timevoid right now."

Kirk grinned widely to indicate he was just joking, but Jan for one wasn't laughing.

"I think Jan may be right about this," Horatio said. "I'm sure you three have got a lot to talk about but business should come first. Jan and Gail have a report to deliver."

"Oh, yes, sir," said Kirk. "Of course, sir. I fully understand."

Jan could hardly resist laughing at Kirk's obsequiousness. He seemed hardly changed at all by his service in time.

Taking Gail by the hand, Kirk led her through the cave entrance and out into the light of day. Pausing briefly, he removed the heavy coat he was wearing and laid it delicately across her bare shoulders. "You must be freezing," he said in a soft tone meant only for her ears.

"Yes, thank you, Kirk, I was."

Jan saw her squeeze his hand. The two of them leaped swiftly ahead, soon outdistancing Horatio and Jan.

"How did we ever get stuck with him?" Jan asked, as they moved down the hillside.

"He was available. The squad he had been serving with—in Tibet of all places—got caught in a snow avalanche. The three others were killed and Kirk survived alone."

"Bad luck for us."

"For them, too. But I thought he was your pal."

"I knew him."

"But didn't like him?"

"No."

"Any specific reason?"

"He's a phony."

"Well, that's nothing particularly extraordinary. That makes four of us in the squad." Horatio chuckled.

Jan didn't join him. Frowning fiercely, he stomped ahead till he was walking alone. It seemed the only viable compromise between separate evils.

Jan shoved a spoonful of beans into his mouth and chewed furiously as though the beans were a tough steak. Across the low table, Horatio puffed contentedly on his pipe. He was holding a book in his hands and apparently reading.

"You know, it could be Indians," said Jan, through his mouthful. "I still think you ought to send me out to see."

"And lose three instead of two? That wouldn't be smart."

"I thought it was your duty to protect the squad."

"Within reason. Nobody can protect another from his own heart."

"What do you mean by that?" Jan glared. "Who do you think you're talking about?"

89

Horatio shrugged and went back to his book.

Jan refused to drop the topic. "Or they could be lost. Kirk has only been here a week. Gail doesn't know the local terrain that well."

"That's why I gave them a compass."

"They could have lost it. Or broken it."

Horatio shut his book on a finger. He sighed deeply and said, "Jan, you and I both know darn well why they're not here and it has nothing to do with broken compasses. So why don't you just shut up, find something to do, and let me alone with my book." The volume was a collection of stories by a man named Kipling. Horatio said he was the only writer who had ever written anything capable of making sense in terms of the real world. Not the best writer—just the most sensible.

Jan shoved another angry mouthful of beans down his throat. He waved his spoon across the table. "I think he's even managed to fool you. I really do."

"Fool me? In what way?"

"With that phoney line of his. You forget I went through the Academy with that guy. I know exactly how two-faced he can be. There's no way of trusting him an inch."

"He told me you two got along all right at the Academy. Was that a lie?"

"No, but I never liked him. I'm only trying to warn you now. So you won't be fooled."

Horatio sighed and dropped his book to the floor with a loud thump. "All right. I see there's no way of avoiding this. Jan, shut your mouth for a few moments because I'm about to deliver a speech."

Jan moaned inwardly but he said, "Yes, sir."

"Good, because the title of my speech is 'The Fellow at Your Back,' and in case you're wondering, the identity of that fellow is Kirk Rayburn. My thesis is that you better learn to love him."

Jan couldn't help laughing.

Horatio ignored him, continuing on. "You say you

couldn't trust him. I'm saying you better learn how. The corps is a mighty big organization, Jan, and I've been part of it longer than any man alive, excepting the Captain. In that time I've had to work beside a goodly assortment of ladies and gentlemen and nearly all of them I have liked. But there were exceptions. A few I have even loathed. But, in nearly every case, like or dislike or even loathe, I came to the conclusion that I loved them."

"Loved them?" Jan thought he might have heard wrong.

"That's what I said, and you want to know why? Because of my back. Because, serving in time, there's always going to come a moment in the stream when you're being hit at from two directions simultaneously and when that occurs you have to be able to turn your back and tell your partner to protect it for you. Whenever you do that, it's got to be an act of faith, and to me faith and love are interchangeable commodities. In the corps, without faith and love, you will soon be a dead man."

"In other words, you want me to act like I trust Kirk even if I don't."

"I never said that. No, sir. I talked about loving and you do not, cannot, fake love. If you're faking, then it means when that moment comes to turn your back you will first hesitate. You will stand a moment too long and you will end up a dead man. I'm willing to trust my back to you, to Gail, and—until something tells me otherwise—to Kirk. You have got to be able to say that, too, Jan, and if you cannot, then I'm going to have to transfer you to another squad."

"I don't want that, Horatio."

"Neither do I. All I ask is that you keep in mind exactly what I'm asking of you. There's no need to like Kirk. But you have to love him. To do that you have to decide the following: is he competent? Can he protect you? His personality is irrelevant to that consideration.

91

It don't matter that he swiped your girl friend from under your nose. If you don't want—"

"She's not my girl friend."

"Shut up and let me finish." He paused for a long moment, then suddenly laughed. "Actually, I guess I am finished." Reaching down, he retrieved his book. "So get out of here," he told Jan. "Go hole up in a corner and make up your mind. Consider what I said, then come back and tell me your decision."

"All right, I will," said Jan.

He did exactly as Horatio directed. Kneeling down upon the hearth in front of the fire, he proceeded to think as hard as he ever had in his life.

A short time later Horatio called his name.

Jan looked up. "Yes?"

"I thought you ought to know: this isn't the first time lately I had to make this speech."

"No?"

"I told it to Gail, too. When she first arrived. It was why I was late picking you up in the field."

"And what did she say?"

"She's here, ain't she?"

"Oh."

So Jan thought some more. He stared into the flames licking high at the fireplace bricks, hoping to glimpse an answer somewhere in there.

Finally, he decided he knew it. He turned around and faced the table. "Horatio?"

"Yes?" He barely glanced up from his book.

"I've made up my mind."

"Good. Let's hear it."

"I'll trust him."

"You're sure?"

"I have no reason not to. He did all right at the Academy. He's not stupid. I don't think he's a coward. Yes, I'm sure."

"I'm glad to hear you say that, Jan."

"Then I can stay?"

"I wouldn't have it any other way."

92

In a scene quickly becoming familiar through repetition, Horatio loomed, a spectral presence in the faint dawn light, when Jan awoke that following morning.

He clutched a suit of clothes in his hands. "Time to go voyaging." He dropped the suit on Jan's chest.

"Yes, sir." The coat was soiled and wrinkled, the shirt worn at both elbows, and the pants sorely in need of pressing. He dressed quickly.

"You've got ten minutes," Horatio said.

Across the room, Jan observed Gail and Kirk also dressing. He wondered how long they had stayed out the night before. Neither looked especially wide awake and he and Horatio had not gone to bed themselves much before midnight.

But Gail and Kirk were not the only ones over there, either. A stranger stood, speaking softly to Horatio. She was middle-aged and undistinguished and dressed in the feminine equivalent of Jan's worn suit.

When he came over to join the others, Horatio took a moment to introduce the stranger. "This is Elinor Bateman," he said. "Professor Elinor Bateman. She'll be going with Jan and Kirk in order to make some observations upstream. I want you to help her in any way possible."

"But we'll be in charge," Kirk wanted made clear. "Not her."

"Jan will be, yes. Gail and I will be handling an assignment in 1955. You and Jan will accompany Professor Bateman to 1963. You'll get a look at a reigning President of the United States but otherwise it's a pretty routine voyage."

"I disagree with that," Elinor Bateman said. "1963 is a fascinating year. Many scholars—I'm one of them—feel that it was during this time that America reached her real peak as a world and national power."

"I'll take 1803 any day," said Horatio.

Elinor smirked. "You would."

Kirk turned to Gail and, in a voice just loud enough

to guarantee that everyone would hear, he said, "I'm sorry we won't be going back together."

"Oh, don't worry," Gail said. "This way you can take good care of Jan."

"Didn't you hear what Horatio said? He put Jan in charge. That means he'll be taking care of me." He smiled.

She laughed. "That should be fascinating to see."

Horatio refused to pretend he hadn't heard. "Nobody in this squad better waste a moment taking care of another. If you can't take care of yourself, put in for a transfer."

"I didn't mean that, Horatio."

"I was sure you didn't, Kirk." Horatio grinned and winked at Jan. "Now let's all shut up and get out of here."

Outside the cabin, it was a bright and delicious spring morning, with songbirds whistling in the branches and a warm wind humming through the leaves. Jan almost hated to be voyaging upstream and leaving such loveliness behind.

He was enjoying his solitary walk through the forest when suddenly Gail left Kirk's side and hurried back to join him. She didn't wait a second before telling him how he ought to be ashamed of what he had done.

"Huh?" said Jan. "What are you talking about? I haven't done anything."

"Then what do you call embarrassing Kirk that way? Really, Jan, you ought to be ashamed. I never knew you were so petty."

"But I didn't—"

"Keep your voice down. You don't have to tell all the world."

"But I don't know what you're talking about."

She smirked. "I suppose you're going to deny what you did. You and Horatio were all alone last night. It doesn't take a genius to figure out what happened. You wouldn't have wasted such a golden opportunity to poison Horatio against Kirk. I don't know what you

94

could have told him. Lies, I suppose. About the Academy."

"I didn't tell him anything," Jan said, with as much dignity as he could manage.

"You didn't talk about Kirk?"

"Not in that way."

She laughed. "Then you admit you did?"

"I don't admit anything."

"Then why—tell me this—why did Horatio choose you to head your group?"

"You'll have to ask him."

"Why should I? I know why. It was because of the lies you told. Kirk has plenty more experience serving in time than you. He made more than a dozen voyages before coming here."

"In one of them, three people died."

Gail looked shocked and horrified. "You didn't tell Horatio that?"

"Why should I? You don't think he forgot."

"That's not fair. That wasn't Kirk's fault. It was an accident—an avalanche."

"How do you know? You weren't there. None of us was. All we have is Kirk's word and if he walked up to me right now and told me my name was Jan Jeroux I'm not sure I'd believe him without checking with someone else first."

"Why, that's a terrible thing to say. That's not fair."

Jan laughed. "Maybe not, but it's a truth."

Gail spun angrily away and ran back to Kirk. Jan watched the two of them talking and grinned bitterly to himself.

If Gail wanted to find things that weren't fair, all she had to do was come and ask him. He'd show her a whole book full of them. And the first chapter would be titled Kirk Rayburn.

CHAPTER ELEVEN

It came as no surprise to Jan when, shortly after their arrival in 1963, Kirk crept over to him and said, in a confidential tone, "I hope you didn't pay attention to anything Gail might have said. She gets a bit carried away sometimes but as far as I'm concerned you're the boss here and that's fair with me."

"You don't think it ought to be you."

"I only want to do my duty to the corps. I'm not chasing after power and glory."

"But what about all those lies? The ones I told Horatio about you?"

Kirk shook his head in stunned disbelief. "Did Gail tell you that? I really don't know where she gets some of these crazy ideas. Not from me. I can guarantee that."

"Sure, Kirk," said Jan, barely resisting an impulse to spit in his face.

"Then we're still friends. Right?" Kirk extended his hand in testimony.

"The same as we always were," said Jan, who managed successfully to pretend he had not noticed the hand.

They had come to a city called Dallas in a state named Texas on the evening of November 21, 1963. Although Jan remained nominally in charge of the party, it was Elinor Bateman who took the lead immediately following their arrival in a conveniently vacant lot. "I've been here before," she told Jan. "I think I can find us a suitable place to stay."

Their old and worn clothing, presumably chosen by Horatio for the usual reasons of anonymity, did not permit a whole lot of leeway in the choice of domicile.

Elinor guided them into a dirty and tired corner of the city, where they first stopped and purchased a suitcase each in a bright pawnshop. Then, around the next corner, they rented adjoining rooms in a dilapidated but clean hotel.

After depositing their empty baggage, they met again in the corridor. Elinor suggested stepping out for a quick meal. Jan and Kirk were agreeable, so she led them to a large drug-store nearby and found them seats at a crowded counter. They ordered hot beef sandwiches, which proved upon delivery to taste even worse than Jan had expected.

After a few tentative bits, Jan shoved the sandwiches aside, drank the glass of milk that had come with it, then asked Elinor why, if this place was a drugstore, it seemed to have everything in the world for sale except drugs.

"Oh, they have them, too," she explained. "An enormous quantity, in fact. You just have to know where to look." Lowering her voice to avoid attracting the unwanted notice of their fellow diners or the various bustling waitresses, she went on: "The economy of this time was predicated upon the assumption that over-production, for everyone meant instant wealth for all. And over-production, of course, required over-consumption and since consumption was confused with wealth, the system seemed to be working remarkably well. It was both America's grandest glory and also a significant aspect in her subsequent decline. Still, I ask you, where else in history can one find a hundred different varieties of sprays, powders, and oils designed for no other purpose than to disguise and conceal the faint natural odor of the human body?"

On their way out of the drugstore, Elinor drew Jan aside and showed him a vast display of the articles she had described. As they wandered through the twisting innards of the store, Jan could not help being impressed —but also more than slightly disgusted—by the multitude of riches he saw. But it was difficult to avoid contrasting the tinsel glitter and glamor of these countless commodities with the wide sweeping fields of the homestead. For the first time in many weeks, he was struck by a painful wave of homesickness. Never before had he felt as far from home as he did now.

Back at the hotel, the three of them descended to a small darkened room adjacent to the central lobby. Here a tired collection of mostly old men sat stiffly about on plastic-covered chairs and couches, while a flickering black-and-gray television screen showed images of times and places far removed from this room. Jan, Kirk, and Elinor watched a local news telecast. The impending visit of the President to the city was the major item described but the old men seemed restless and disinterested. Several unfurled newspapers and one cried out for the station to be changed, but Elinor said she was interested and the man relented, apparently out of respect for her sex. (She was the only woman present in the room.) The news program was very brief, however, and was immediately followed by a puzzling program in which various people were expected to perform tricks and stunts in return for money. In the portion Jan watched, a young woman was asked to throw a selection of cream and berry pies in her husband's face, while simultaneously balancing a pail of water in the palm of her hand. Should she drop the pail or fail to place a sufficient number of pies where directed, the money would be withheld from her.

Jan got up and left before the final outcome was determined. His sympathies lay entirely with the poor, pie-encrusted husband and the assault upon his face (and dignity) had become too painful to watch.

The room he and Kirk were sharing was bare of furniture and uncarpeted. The flowering wallpaper sagged in the corners and was peeled almost everywhere. Jan flopped down on the narrow bed and scanned the front pages of the newspaper he had picked up below. Again, the visit of the President received top billing.

A flurry of taps sounded at the door and was followed, moments later, by the appearance of Kirk. He poked his head through the door and let his eyes dart from left to right.

"You alone?" he asked Jan.

"I don't know who else would be here?"

"I thought Bateman."

"Isn't she watching television?"

"Yeah, but I thought she snuck up here when I left."

"No, I haven't seen her."

This seemed to satisfy Kirk and he finally came all the way inside, shutting the door at his back.

Jan asked, "What's up?"

"Oh, nothing. I was just bored." Kirk came over and sat on the edge of the bed. His attitude was strenuously relaxed and unextraordinary.

"Are you sure there's nothing?" said Jan.

"Oh, sure. But I was just wondering. You know how it is. Wondering why she's here."

"Elinor? Didn't Horatio tell you? She's a professor doing research."

"That's what I was wondering about. You know that's not true."

"I don't know any such thing."

Kirk peered at Jan quizzically, then finally shrugged. "I suppose you don't know. But then you haven't been around the timestream as long as I have."

Impatiently, Jan dropped his newspaper. "Are you going to tell me what you're talking about?"

"Well, that's the problem. It's really not something I can talk about. It's nothing I can prove. But I believe it. I want you to know that. I've seen too much not to believe."

"Believe what?" Jan said. "I don't have any idea of what you're talking about."

"I think she's here to perform an assignment none of the rest of us can do. I've seen it happen before. When I was in Tibet, the squad leader used to do it all the time. I remember one time when he made me shove an Englishman into a pool of dirty water to keep him from making an appointment with some Germans who were there at the same time."

"Why should anyone want to do that?" Jan's voice reflected his concern. He could not help recollecting William Waite and the dandy he was supposed to meet.

"Don't ask me that," Kirk said, "because I don't know. All I can say is I have my theories and even if half of them are incorrect I still don't like what's left over. I bet if you keep a close eye on her tomorrow, you'll see something you don't like, either."

Jan was confused. Why was Kirk telling him all this? What was he trying to prove? "She knows what she's doing. I don't think she'd do anything wrong."

"Is changing history right?" asked Kirk.

Jan laughed. "You can't change history."

"Who told you that?"

"Why, Horatio. Why else?"

Kirk smirked and shook his head sadly. "And you believe him?"

Jan was defensive. "Yes, I do."

"Then all I can tell you is to watch what happens tomorrow. I'd bet a million dollars I'm right. I'd bet another million that Horatio knows the real facts, exactly what's going on, but he isn't about to tell any of us. Something's going on here—something that really stinks."

"You don't have any proof. You said so yourself. All you know is that your old squad leader once knocked a guy into a pool of water."

"That wasn't the only time. I saw it happen before and after, too. Sure you don't want to bet?"

"Money doesn't mean anything to us."

"Then I'll tell you what," said Kirk. "Tomorrow, after you've watched Bateman and seen what—".

He never finished. Just then, the door popped open and Elinor entered. She looked at Jan, then at Kirk.

"Oh, here you are. I was worried you might have wandered off when I noticed you both were gone. It's late. I thought we ought to go to bed."

"I'm not tired," Kirk said. He looked meaningfully in Jan's direction.

"I'm not, either," said Jan.

"Then I guess none of us are." Elinor dropped down on the floor with a loud sigh. "I guess it must be the sheer excitement of the occasion. Here I am, I've been back here several times before—I've seen this man, the President—and yet it's still history happening right under my nose and I just don't want to sleep and miss a minute of it. I'm surprised, though, that it affects you fellows the same way. Most corpsmen get to be pretty jaded."

"Well, we're young," said Kirk. "We're innocent."

"I guess that must be it," she agreed. Then she went right on talking. She was still going at it when Jan fell asleep on the bed.

By noon, Jan stood among the thick crowd that filled the whole of the concrete sidewalk from the gutter clear back to the buildings behind. Along with everyone else, he was eagerly anticipating the arrival of the procession bearing the President of the United States but, still disturbed by Kirk's charges of the night before, he kept an eye closely fixed upon Elinor.

She, in turn, seemed concerned with nothing beyond the events of the moment. She had not ventured out of his sight since they had first come here, nor had she tried. Kirk had moved farther forward into the crowd, however, and Jan hadn't seen him for some time.

"He should be here soon," Jan said. "If he isn't, I think this crowd is going to spill out into the street."

"He's got twenty minutes yet. But don't worry. The police back here were mean when they had to be."

"But why would they have to be?"

"Assassination."

"But that never happened."

102

"Don't you remember Garfield?"

"But that was a long time before this."

"Not that long. Why don't we try to move up? I don't want Kirk to get lost. Maybe we can find him."

Jan was agreeable but moving forward through the crowd proved no easy process. Still, by painstakingly stepping around those people who refused to budge, they at last reached a place from where they could easily see the street itself. They had failed to catch sight of Kirk. Jan was worried but Elinor did not think it was anything to be concerned about. She glanced at her watch and announced that the President was due in twelve minutes. Jan wondered at the mood of the crowd, which seemed to swing restlessly between loud enthusiasm and silent anticipation. There was a peculiar sense of anxiety in the air. The absence of street traffic only added to the strangeness of the scene. Of all the qualities of the age, it was these loud, filth-belching automobiles that puzzled Jan the most. They seemed to serve no real purpose. As transportation, they were too powerful, as conveniences, too ornate, and as aesthetic objects, totally lacking in beauty or grace.

Then Elinor announced: "I forgot something I wanted to see. I'll be right back." She turned toward the crowd.

Jan grabbed her shoulder. "What is it?"

She shook her head and smiled. "Nothing important. I'll be right back."

"But don't you think I should go with you?"

"Why, no. Why should you? Stay here and look for Kirk. I said I'd be right back." And she stepped away without waiting for him to protest further.

The moment she disappeared into the crowd, Kirk suddenly materialized at his elbow. "See? What did I tell you? There she goes."

"Where have you been?" said Jan.

"Nearby. Watching. Come on—let's see where she goes."

"But—"

"Come on. This is more important than any stupid President."

So Jan allowed Kirk to draw him back into the crowd. It was easier going this way, against the grain, than trying to move forward. Jan kept catching faint glimpses of Elinor and then losing sight of her again almost right away. But Kirk seemed to know where he was going. He hardly even bothered to look up.

At last, they emerged from the thicket of the crowd. Rising in front of them was a large building of perhaps six or seven floors. Kirk tugged Jan forward until they could see through the doors. They were just in time to see Elinor stepping into an elevator.

"Let's catch her," said Kirk, clearly intending to follow.

But something told Jan to resist. He refused to budge. "No."

"But don't you want to see what she's up to?"

Jan felt himself getting angry. "No, I don't want to see. Right now, I don't care. We were sent here to do an assignment and this isn't it." He started to back away. "Come on before we miss the President."

This time it was Kirk who resisted. "No." He drew away from Jan. "I'm going into that building."

"You do and I'm telling Horatio."

"You wouldn't."

"Why not? I'm in charge of this party. You disobey an order of mine and it's the same as disobeying one of his."

Kirk laughed strangely. "You're afraid to find out. That's what it is. You know as well as I do something rotten is going on around here."

"I know what my assignment is." He stepped deliberately toward the crowd. "You better come."

Kirk did. As he accompanied Jan through the crowd, he kept silent.

But they were too late anyway. By the time they reached the street, the President's motorcade had passed.

Elinor joined them a few moments later. She said, "I

104

saw him from back there. Wasn't it something? What did you think?"

"I thought it was very impressive," Kirk said, casting a meaningful look at Jan."

"Yeah," said Jan. "Me, too. It was history come alive."

CHAPTER TWELVE

They came more frequently now: the voyages. At times as many as three and four brief excursions up the stream in the course of a single week. Sometimes it was Kirk and Jan, Gail and Horatio; at other times the groups were reversed and it was Kirk and Horatio, Gail and Jan. A few times, outsiders—scholars like Elinor Bateman—joined them. Most often, however, it was just Kirk and Gail, Jan and Horatio. The squad seemed to function best this way and Horatio said that was his primary responsibility as a leader. "I also hear confessions, hold hands, pronounce marriages, cuss out, and play poker. But I try to do everything efficiently. And that's the key."

Jan and Gail did not get along. The truth was as simple as that. In the beginning, he had a couple times attempted to apologise to her for whatever it was she felt he had done wrong but had not been granted a hearing. He assumed she had never forgiven him his early—though largely imagined—transgressions against Kirk and he finally decided that if she was going to be that bullheaded then he could do the same. The result was that, while they willingly protected each other's back when serving in time, they seldom spoke otherwise.

As far as Kirk was concerned, Jan didn't like him. A few hours after their return from 1963, Kirk had approached Jan furtively and asked:

"Did you tell him?"

"Tell who?"

"Horatio, of course. About what I said. What I did."

"Not yet, I haven't."

"But you intend to?"

"If what you said was true, don't you think I should?"

"No." Kirk shook his head excitedly. "I was wrong. I got to thinking about it and the whole thing is crazy. You can't change time. Why, if you could, the whole future would be changed, too, and that's never happened."

"What about Elinor?"

"Who knows?" Kirk shrugged as if the question had never possessed the faintest consequence. "Probably she had to go to the bathroom. I mean, how could she change history by going into a schoolbook factory?"

"That was a question I intended asking you. And Horatio."

"Well, let's just forget it, okay? It was stupid of me—crazy—that's all. Don't say anything to Horatio or any of them. You know he'd have me transferred if he found out and it would ruin my career."

Jan finally said, "All right."

"You promise?"

"I said, all right, didn't I?"

But he didn't like him. Nor did he trust him. Oh, Jan trusted Kirk in the limited sense of being willing to risk his life in his hands, but he wouldn't have trusted him an inch in the real sense of being friends. But, as Horatio said, you didn't have to like a man to love him and that was the philosophy which had come to guide Jan's relations with Kirk Rayburn.

But he didn't see much of those two anyway. When they were not voyaging, they were most often out in the woods together. Kirk had built a small treehouse in the lower branches of a strong pine and while it was too cold for sleeping the long summer daylight hours could all be spent out there.

As a result, Horatio and Jan spent a great deal of time together, and that was the thing—next to actually serving in time—that Jan liked best. Horatio had even shown Jan how to operate the time traveling equipment and—vaguely—how and why it worked. This was an honor he had not as yet bestowed upon the other two and Jan was thoroughly aware of the favoritism he was being shown.

In the cabin late one summer evening, Horatio lit the logs in the fireplace, then turned away from the rapidly roaring flames

"What are you thinking about?" he asked Jan. This was often the spark that set off hours-long conversations between them.

"I was trying to decide what my favorite time is," said Jan, "but it's really hard to say. You know, trying to answer the question of when I'd like to live if the choice was offered me."

"That's an easy question to answer."

"For you maybe, but not for me. I know some parts of the stream I like much better than other parts. The twentieth century, for instance, is a lot less interesting than the nineteenth or the twenty-first, and some parts of the nineteenth cannot compare with all of the eighteenth."

"I thought you'd say something like that." He put his hands behind his back and waved them at the fire. "You're still just a homestead kid."

"Something wrong with that?" Jan could not help bristling somewhat.

"Not a darn thing. All it means is that you're going to prefer wide-open country with as few people clogging up the scenery as possible."

"Isn't that what America is really about? The frontier."

"Perhaps, but I think it depends on how you define that word. A big city slum can be a frontier just as easily as a stretch of arid desert, and we all know America has had her share of both those commodities."

"But you dress like a frontiersman. You even talk like one."

"Well, sure. Why not? It's an image and I have fun wearing it. Yet if you were to stick me down in the middle of twentieth century New York or Chicago, I think I'd be as much at home as in the Dodge City of

1870. You're just not a city boy, Jan. It's why I take Kirk with me whenever I have to voyage up that way. Kirk blends in real well with all those brownstones and tenements, and you don't."

It was exceedingly rare for Horatio to talk about their work or about the squad. Jan was thoroughly impressed by the significance of the moment but knew enough not to let Horatio see how he felt. "Don't you think you ought to give me a chance to learn?"

"Oh, I will. In good time."

"Then how about telling me what it is you like about the cities? I'm afraid that's the part I really don't understand."

"What I like about them?" Horatio visibly pondered the question. "I guess you could say it's the stink, the reek, the odor of life. I hate what you might call the dead air towns. In New York in 1840—or in 1925, for that matter—that stink surrounds you everywhere. It fills the air and saturates your very skin. What you might call it—to stretch the metaphor clean out of shape—is the lifeblood of the city flowing through the veins of its downtown streets. By 1970, though, that stink is gone. In Los Angeles, it is never present. In San Francisco or Chicago, it never wholly disperses. I hate the places where it ain't and I love them where it is. That's about all I can tell you."

"Then when is your time? The one you'd choose to live in forever?"

"Why? Finally make up your own mind?"

"I think so," Jan said. "I think what I'd pick would be a small farm. In Illinois or Indiana. A corn farm with a few milk cows. Say, in 1840."

Horatio grinned. "See? What did I tell you? A homestead boy. But, on this farm, would you live alone?"

"I don't suppose I could. I'd have to hire some hands to help me with the harvest, that sort of thing."

Horatio clucked his tongue. "No good. Help was hard to come by in those years. Why should a fellow go to work for another when all he had to do was walk

110

a few miles to the west and have a place of his own? No, sir, the best bet for you is to find a wife quick and have plenty of children."

Jan laughed. "That's really trying, but okay—why not?"

"Why not indeed?" Horatio agreed. "At least as far as you're concerned, but for me that kind of life would be boring. Not unpleasant, mind you, but I've been voyaging up and down the timestream for too long to be satisfied with tranquility. I've got to have a share of the action. That's why I'd pick San Francisco. Before the big quake—the first one—let's make it 1888. Put me down there and I'd spread deep roots and live the life of Horatio Nextor, true and whole and quite complete."

"I wish you could," Jan said.

"You ain't alone. But I can't. It's impossible."

"Couldn't you retire there?"

"I'll never retire."

"Why not?"

Horatio shook his head in such a way as to indicate that the particular subject was closed. Then he moved immediately into another area: "You know, Jan, you never told me about your family. Knowing how the homesteaders are organized, I'm surprised, because you must have been close to them."

"I told you about my Uncle Phineas."

"Your uncle, sure, but never your father or mother."

"Well, that's because I never knew them."

"Dead?"

"I don't know. Nobody ever told me for certain."

"And you never asked?"

"Sure, I did. When I was a boy, I asked all the time. I asked my sister, everyone, but she didn't know and the others wouldn't answer me straight out. Finally, Uncle Phineas took me aside and said I had a right to know. He told me they had both gone away right after I was born and neither would ever likely be coming back. He said, when they left, they planned on coming back but since they hadn't in so long a time I shouldn't start counting on it."

"That's good advice. Did he tell you where they went?"

"He was always mysterious about that. If I asked him straight out, he changed the subject. I think he knew, though."

Horatio pondered this for a moment, as though it were a mystery to be solved through deductive methods. "I think your mother's dead."

Jan was puzzled by the certainty of his tone. "How come? Did you know her?"

"Well, because if she was alive, being a mother, she would surely have come back to see you sometime. With a father, it's different, because he's more selfish and apt to get so wrapped up in his own affairs that he loses sight of everything else until it's way too late."

"Then you know my father? He's in the corps?"

"I didn't say that. I said it's possible he's alive."

"I see, but—"

Horatio held up a hand, indicating that this subject, too, had now been exhausted. "Jan, there's something I want to ask you while we're alone. A favor."

"Sure, Horatio."

"Have you noticed Gail lately? That she's been acting rather odd and funny? As if something with big sharp teeth were lodged way inside her, eating away at her innards."

Jan shrugged. "She seems the same to me."

"Well, I'd like you to try and find out."

"Me?" Jan nearly laughed. "She won't talk to me."

"There's a mission scheduled for tomorrow. A routine trip upstream to 1965. I'll take Kirk with me. You and Gail will stay here alone and I want you to try."

"I tell you it's useless."

"Try. You might be surprised. I wouldn't normally ask someone to do this. It smacks of spying. But I have a feeling this may be important."

"How so?"

"If I knew the answer to that, I wouldn't need your help."

The next day, true to his word, Horatio took Kirk by the arm and decamped to the cave and the timestream beyond. Alone with Gail, Jan occupied his hands as night fell by cooking a dinner of venison and fresh corn. Gail ate silently. Jan was cursing Horatio to himself. This whole thing was silly and pointless and, what was worse, embarrassing. She would never talk to him—she didn't need him.

Then Gail burst into tears. She laid her head on the low table and wept soundlessly.

Jan, stunned, could do nothing more than hover over her, an empty plate in his hands.

"Is—is something wrong?" he finally asked.

She murmured from below: "No—no, nothing."

Hesitantly, he dropped down beside her and placed a cautious hand upon her shoulder. "Can I help?"

"No."

He gathered up his courage: "You could tell me."

"No, it won't help."

He was nearly more relieved than not. "Well, if you don't want to—"

She raised her head suddenly. Her eyes were red and her cheeks streaked with tears. "It's not that I don't want to. It's just that I don't know how."

"Try. Just find the beginning and start there."

"I can't. Because—well, it's just too big. It's not one thing, it's everything. The corps, the timestream—nothing is the way I wanted it to be."

"I don't understand." And he did not; until this moment he had thought Gail was as happy in the corps as he was.

"You wouldn't. You're ignorant. You didn't have the preconceptions I had. You hadn't heard about the corps all your life, and dreamed about it, and read every history book you could find in hopes that someday you would be there. You never did all that, only to find out the whole thing stinks."

"History can't be just like the books. The books don't have room to show the warts."

"That's easy enough to say."

He shrugged. "It's the truth."

"But I don't want it to be the truth. I want the lies. I like the lies. I want to think of Thomas Jefferson as a tall and wonderful and great man, not find out, when I voyage to 1803, that he's just—well, just like everyone else."

Standing up, Jan crossed to the fireplace where, squatting upon the hearth, he pretended to arrange the logs. Turning back to Gail, he said, "I think your problem is you're trying to judge the world on some private moral scale. What you have to do is learn to deal with it as it is."

"That's easy to say, too."

"Easier to say than do, that's for sure."

"Yes." She sighed. "I suppose you're right. But it's just that—well, you tell me. What is this whole thing about?"

"The corps?"

"Right. What are we doing back here?"

"Collecting history." As he spoke, he suddenly realized that this was something he had really not thought of before. "Studying the past so that we can better understand the present—and the future."

Gail was unmoved. "You don't believe that, do you?"

"Why shouldn't I?"

"Because who cares about history? Besides us, I mean."

"People like Elinor Bateman."

"Are you sure? How do you know?"

He abruptly realized that he had not been paying close enough attention to what she was saying. He became instantly suspicious. "What is this? Is it something Kirk told you?"

114

Their brief intimacy was suddenly gone. Gail looked deliberately away. "Oh, shut up."

Jan climbed to his feet. He understood now. "So that's what it is. I should have known. Has he been telling you crazy things? About changing time? I bet—"

She met his angry gaze. "He told me nothing."

Jan loomed over her like an avenging angel. "If he has, if that's why you're so upset, then I'll—"

She jumped to her feet. "You won't do a thing. You'll keep your mouth shut and that's all. I told you a lot more than I ever should have. I trusted you. If you breathe one word of this to Horatio—to anyone—I swear I'll . . . I'll . . ."

"Well, don't you understand Kirk is wrong? He doesn't know what he's talking about."

"I never said anything about Kirk. All I wanted was some help, from you, and not a lot of accusations."

He realized he had been taking the wrong tact with her. Now, too late, he tried to apologise: "I'm sorry. I shouldn't have threatened you. All I wanted was to help—really.

"Then you can help by forgetting what I said. That's all I ask."

He sighed. "All right, I will."

So, when Horatio returned from 1965 and he and Jan were alone, Jan told him, "I talked to her. She's just depressed that's all."

"You don't know why?"

"She's having trouble adjusting to the realities of the timestream."

"And that's it? It's not Kirk? If it is, I'll have him transfered or worse in a minute."

"He has nothing to do with it," Jan said.

He didn't like saying that. The question was, to whom did he owe his deepest loyalty? To Gail? To Horatio? To the corps?

Of course, through his answer, he had already decided that question. But was he right?

CHAPTER THIRTEEN

Horatio pawed through boxes filled with shirts and skirts, caps and gowns, boots and bustles in search of appropriate attire for the squad's latest pair of impending voyages into the timestream. As was often the case, the hour had barely cleared dawn. Watching Horatio, Jan yawned deeply and struggled to shake the sleep from his eyes.

"Ah, this will do just right," Horatio muttered, emerging from a box clutching a dark suit and bright ruffled silk shirt. These garments were the sort Jan associated with the prancing dandies of the mid-nineteenth century South and he hoped they were not intended for him. Horatio had already announced that his own buckskin would do, and Jan wanted to go with him.

Horatio threw the suit and shirt to Kirk and told him to put them on. Jan smiled in relief.

"And this'll be for you, Jan," Horatio added a moment later. He held up a pair of frayed buckskin britches, which Jan gratefully accepted. "Now where's that lovely little gown I was saving for Gail?" Horatio returned to his search.

"Wait a minute," said Kirk.

Horatio looked up, blinking at the unexpected interruption. Kirk hadn't budged. He held the suit and shirt in his hands. "Something wrong?" Horatio said. "Your suit don't fit?"

"It's not that," said Kirk. "I was just wondering. Where do you intend on sending us?"

Horatio shook his head in astonishment. Clearly,

the bluntness of Kirk's question disturbed him. Still, all he said was, "How come you want to know that?"

"Simple curiosity." Kirk plainly did not intend to retreat an inch. "I'd like to know."

"You would, huh?" Horatio considered this puzzling fact. Finally, shrugging, he said, "I guess there's no reason you shouldn't know. The fact is, among my belongings, I recently came across a pair of tickets to the March 1849 inaugural of James Buchanan. He ain't too terribly interesting a man himself, though his inability to act during the slave uprisings of his second term did tend to guarantee the end to that institution, but I did think it might be worthwhile to pick up a few firsthand impressions of men like Clay, Calhoun, and Webster, who were then in their declining years. As long as Jan and I were slated for an assignment, I thought I'd have you you two go out at the same time."

"And where is it you and Jan are going?"

Horatio hesitated before answering, but again it was clear he could find no reason to object: "To New York City. August 1776."

"With George Washington."

"Right. We're going to see his end."

"I'd like to go there with you," Kirk said.

This time Horatio's expression was one of genuine shock, but instead of blowing up or questioning Kirk further, he turned his gaze upon Gail. She said nothing but lowered her eyes and peered carefully at the floor.

"Trouble?" Horatio asked Kirk.

Kirk flared angrily: "My private life is my own business, isn't it? All I asked for was a change of assignment. You can either say yes or no."

Horatio nodded, properly chastened. "You're right. Sometimes I've got too big a nose. But the fact is it ain't my policy to go switching assignments for any personal or private reason. Jan is my choice to go with me to 1776 and that is that."

For the first time, Gail spoke: "I wish you'd make an exception this time, Horatio."

"Nope." He was firm. "I don't care if you two are mad at each other. You can still do your work."

"This doesn't involve liking or disliking," Gail said. "It means I wouldn't trust him—" she waved vaguely at Kirk "—to guard my back."

Horatio was very serious. "You mean that?"

"I do. It's possible I may change my mind later, but not right now."

"You know that means I'll have to transfer one or the other of you?"

"I know that."

"And you want it?"

"No, but I can't help my own feelings."

"Mind telling me what it's all about?"

"Yes, I do mind."

"Kirk?"

"It's private."

Horatio sighed, rubbing his chin thoughtfully. You've both been good," he finally said. "I don't want to lose a good man out of my squad because of something that may turn out to be temporary. My first inclination is to suspend the missions, get one of you out here as quickly as possible, and find me a new man. But I'm not going to do that yet. I may have to, but not now. Jan, pass that buckskin over to Kirk. Kirk, you trade with Jan. We're going to make the switch this time but I won't do it again. Understand that? Something's going to have to happen between you two or one goes."

Kirk nodded tightly. "I understand."

"Gail?"

"Me, too," she said softly.

Once they returned to their hotel following an afternoon of sightseeing in and around the Capitol, Gail lost whatever vague animation she had previously possessed and went straight over to the big canopied bed and, without bothering to undress lay down upon the heavy quilts.

"Draw the curtains," she told Jan. "I don't have the strength."

Is something wrong?"

"I have a headache, that's all."

"Is there something I can do?"

"You can go away and leave me alone."

He sighed, went over, and closed the curtains. He turned back toward the door. "Are you sure I can't get you something?"

Her voice, from inside the curtains, was muffled: "Just go."

"You don't want to talk?"

What about?"

"Kirk. Your troubles."

"We haven't had any troubles."

He opened the door and went out. "If you say so." Outside, the day was bright and crisp, a true spring day at the beginning of March. The air was as clean and pure as that found high in the Rockies. He drew vast quantities of it down into his lungs. He forgot all about Gail and Kirk. Life was too sweet for worrying about others.

They had arrived in Washington that morning shortly after dawn and, once safely registered in one of the city's better hotels, had immediately walked to the vicinity of the Capitol to await the arrival of the new President. The crowd gathered to view the inaugural was surprisingly sparse and well-behaved. To Jan who only a few weeks before had gone with Horatio to attend Andrew Jackson's first inaugural in 1829, the contrast between the staid dignity of the present occasion and the roaring excitement of the other could not have been more obvious. James Buchanan arrived promptly at noon in the company of the outgoing President, James K. Polk. Unlike most such men, Polk who had voluntarily relinquished the Presidency after a single highly successful term, appeared far happier and more relieved than the rather dour Buchanan. And with good reason, Jan thought. Polk could look back upon a string of real accomplishments, the most enduring of which had been the acquisitions of both Texas and Oregon without the need for war. Buchanan, on the other hand, had nothing ahead of him but war, rebellion, and eventual personal disgrace through impeachment.

Chief Justice Roger B. Taney soon stepped forward to swear in Buchanan as the nation's ninth chief executive. The President's address, which followed, was delivered in a soft, halting manner that made listening difficult. As far as Jan could determine, the speech was a rather tepid pledge to work with Congress in attempting to settle the growing differences between North and South. To Jan, these words were more depressive than impressive, but then he and Gail, alone among those present, knew fully of the utter futility of such wasted rhetoric and of the inevitability of future conflict.

After the conclusion of Buchanan's address, Jan suggested they wander down to the Senate to see if they might be allowed inside the Senate galleries, if only briefly. Gail rather listlessly agreed and the two of them soon discovered that entrance was no problem. Down in the chamber below, they watched the newly inaugurated Vice-President, William Butler, presiding. Gail quietly pointed out the many historical luminaries present, men like Clay, Calhoun, Webster, Benton, and Lewis Cass. Jan was amazed that so many men of so much ability had been unable to devise any means of preventing the terrible events that were soon to befall the nation. Gail said they were old and tired and besides some violent end to slavery was perhaps inevitable once the cotton gin was introduced in the thirties. Better now, she said, than later when it would probably have spread as an institution through the gulf states and into Texas. Jan was more impressed by some of the younger Senators present, men who would play significant roles during the healing years of Lincoln. Gail pointed out Seward, Chase, Douglas, and Jefferson Davis. Every great historical figure of the age seemed present in this one room, excepting Lincoln, who was over in the House, and Robert E. Lee.

After the Senate recessed, Jan suggested a tour of

the town but Gail said she didn't feel well and wanted to go back to the hotel and lay down.

So they did and she did and now Jan was alone again. He liked it here. Not only was the air exceptionally clean, but the city of Washington itself was a welcome halfway point between the muddy village of its early years and the great sagging metropolis it was to become. It was a town of broad, tree-lined avenues, considerable open space, and large neat houses. It was also very much a Southern city and for every free white face he passed there seemed to be two additional black captive ones.

So Jan wasn't surprised when he turned a corner and ran right into a slave auction. High upon a wooden platform stood two dark figures. One was a tall man dressed in tattered overalls and the other was a boy of ten or twelve.

From a combination of curiosity and disgust, Jan stepped into the crowd gathered beneath the block. The auctioneer's voice ran swift and shrill through the air and it took Jan a moment to comprehend that the boy was being auctioned off alone. The price reached five hundred dollars and continued to rise.

Jan turned to the man nearest him; "But isn't that his father?"

"Huh? Who?"

"The tall black man. The slave. His father—or his older brother?"

The man laughed. "Now how in hell should I know something like that?"

"But doesn't it matter? Shouldn't somebody ask him?"

"You want to ask him, you ask him. I'm not going up there. He might bite off my hand." For some reason, the man seemed to think that was very funny and he laughed heartily.

Jan moved angrily away. The price on the boy leaped to a thousand dollars and continued to climb in steady increments of a hundred dollars each. Jan was surprised by the active, spirited bidding. He had never realized slavery was such a thriving institution this late in time. Pressing relentlessly forward, he soon stood directly beneath the auction block.

What he wished he could do was enter the bidding himself. If he could somehow manage to purchase both of them, father and son, then he could grant them immediate freedom. The boy was beginning to cry. Jan could see big tears glistening on his cheeks. The man laid a steady hand on his son's shoulder and pressed firmly down. The boy looked up, smiled dimly, and ceased crying. He wiped his eyes and struggled manfully to match his father's expression of unyielding pride.

Jan dug through his pockets but found no more than a mere hundred dollars. The bidding had now reached fourteen hundred. Unable to help, all he could do was stare at the boy's red squinting eyes as he fought to hold back the tears.

In final disgust, Jan turned away. There was nothing more he wanted to see here. He passed a man who suddenly cried out, "Eighteen hundred," but he refused to listen.

The beauty of the day was surely spoiled now.

He tried to continue his wanderings, but there didn't seem to be any use. It was almost as if the city had become suddenly buried beneath a thick dark cloud. It seemed every corner he turned brought him face-to-face with richly decked-out men (and women) bustling about in the company of slaves. Once he recognized the ancient and stately figure of South Carolina Senator John C. Calhoun tottering slowly amid a crowd of open admirers. A pair of black servants helped support his withered figure. Jan knew that Calhoun was the most impressive defender slavery was ever to have. As a result, the sight of this ugly and wasted man disgusted him and he hurried on.

At last he was forced to admit that he had seen way too much of Washington, D.C., 1849. Besides, it was almost time for the inaugural ball and he would have to hurry back to the hotel to ensure that Gail was dressed to go.

Fortunately, his wanderings had carried him almost in a full circle and the hotel was close-by. Entering the lobby, he pushed through the thick crowd gathered there. Every hotel in the city was booked past capacity and the most recent arrivals had been forced to spend their days and nights in the lobbies. He and Gail had been very lucky to get a room even at the excessive rate they were paying.

Climbing the staircase, Jan passed a lone slave who, spying Jan's approach, darted out of the way and bowed after him. Jan could not help himself. He turned, burning with anger, and called out: "Don't do that. You're as good a man as I am. You don't have to bow."

But the slave, if he heard, gave no indication.

It was the change that puzzled Jan the most. The whole mood of the city had changed since morning. He didn't understand it—he wasn't sure he wanted to.

He muttered a quick curse at Kirk Rayburn for forcing him to come to this ugly time when he might right now be back in 1776 with Horatio, watching George Washington pay the price for choosing to lead a rebellion twenty years before the country was ready to accept it. (Or France to assist it.)

Back in the room, he discovered Gail soundly asleep in the bed. Waking her angrily, he said to get dressed and hurry. She told him not to go giving her orders, she wasn't his slave.

She seemed puzzled when he laughed long and hard in response.

When they reached the White House door, Jan removed the pair of inaugural tickets from his pocket and showed them to the tall black man who stood waiting to examine them. Inside, a band was playing spiritedly and he could see the tops of dancing heads.

"Come on," he said to Gail, drawing her forward. "Let's get on inside."

"Sir?" said the black man.

Jan paused. "Yes, what is it?"

The man seemed oddly flustered and upset. He kept looking from the tickets to Jan, then back again, as if the two could not possibly belong together. "Would you mind waiting here a moment, sir? I'll be right back."

"Those tickets are mine," Jan said. "You don't think I stole them, do you?"

"No, sir. Of course not, sir. It's nothing like that. I just have to—to ask a question. I'll be right back. Please wait." Then he hurried off toward a small alcove to the right of the main foyer. Jan watched him go.

"Now what's wrong?" Gail said. Her tone indicated she thought the fault had to be Jan's.

"I haven't the slightest idea. I know it's nothing I did."

"You let him get away with our tickets. That's one thing. Now he'll come back and say he's never seen us before and we'll be out on our ears." She folded her arms across her chest, clearly satisfied she had uncovered the mystery if not its motive. "You just wait."

But it didn't turn out that way at all. The black man returned in the flash of another moment and he was accompanied by a pair of hefty, gnarled white men. One was packing a visible revolver in his belt. They both glared at Jan.

One of the white men was holding Jan's tickets in his fist. He shook them angrily. "Is this your idea of a joke? You trying to pull something funny here?"

Unable to understand what could possibly be going on, Jan decided to play honest. "The only thing I'm trying to pull is to attend this ball. If I have to stand here and answer any more ridiculous questions, I won't make it."

"No, you won't." The man didn't seem disturbed by this concept. "But you're not going an inch until you explain this here." Again, he shook the tickets.

"I'm afraid I don't have the slightest idea of what you're talking about," said Jan.

The man wrinkled his brow. His partner circled surreptitiously until he stood between Jan and the door. Then the first man showed the tickets. "You don't understand this?"

Jan read the information printed on the tickets. Then he looked at the man's cold stare and unable to find any answers any place he read the tickets once more. "I still don't know what you mean."

"Then maybe you do know this much: whose house is this? Who's the President of the United States?"

"Why, James Buchanan, who else?"

"You think that's who it is?"

"Why, of course."

"And these tickets? Whose name does it say here? Read it."

Jan read carefully, as if there might be some possibility of error. "It says just what I said—James Buchanan."

"Jack, can we have your help?" The man spoke to his circling colleague. "What's the President's name? Who do we work for?"

"Zach Taylor. General Taylor."

"Thank you. And, Benjamin—" he meant the black man, who seemed more nervous than ever now "—could we have your considered judgment? What's the name of your boss?"

"The same as the President. Zachery Taylor."

"And before him?"

"Why, President Polk, of course."

"Any Buchanan?"

"Only Mr. Secretary Buchanan."

"Was he ever President?"

"No, sir."

The man turned back to Jan, threw up his arms and let them fall. "You seem to be a minority of one here, my friend. If Buchanan is the President, he has forgotten to tell anyone but you."

"I—I—" said Jan. "What are you trying to prove? Is this supposed to be funny?"

126

The man pointed toward the alcove from which he had first emerged. "I think you better come along with Jack and me for a little chat." His face was stern and no hint of any possible joke clouded his expression.

Jan looked desperately around for Gail. She whispered, "We better go. I think they'd kill us if we didn't."

"Yes," said Jan. "But what can—?"

"Who knows?" She drew him toward the alcove. "Come on and let's find out."

Jan went along, too stunned to protest, but he wasn't sure he really wanted to find out. Something was awfully wrong here. He had sensed it first on his trip through the streets and now he was sure of it. Something awfully, terribly, dreadfully wrong.

But what?

CHAPTER FOURTEEN

Horatio wasn't there.

By the third day, Jan became convinced that futher hope was useless. Horatio wasn't here and he wasn't going to be here. If anyone was going to do anything about what had happened, then that person was going to have to be Jan himself.

So he stood up, went over, and shut down the time traveling equipment. He picked up the old musket he had been holding for three days and carried it out of the cave with him. Then, for the first time since returning from 1849, he walked through the light of day and finally reached the cabin.

Gail was seated at the table, eating. When he entered, she looked up, smiling in hopeful anticipation.

"I gave up," Jan said, slumping to the floor. In three days, he had not slept except in occasional fits and starts. He was exhausted, too beat to move, and the trouble was he still didn't dare sleep.

"Then he's dead," she said.

"Yes."

"If you want I could go down there and watch for him. You know, you don't have to do it all alone. And that gun—I still don't see why you need it."

He was too tired to explain—not that he would have told her anything in any event—so he simply shook his head.

"You've got to get some sleep."

"There isn't time."

"Why not?"

"We've got things to do."

"What?"

"I haven't decided yet."

"Well, if you ever do, don't forget to let me know. I used to be a member of this squad, too, at one time."

"I remember," he said, controlling his temper. Getting mad wouldn't help. It was plain Gail was frightened and worried herself. She was simply masking her real feelings beneath a concealing barrage of false ones.

After a while, she said, "Are you sure I can't go down there? He might be hurt, unable to move."

"I shut down the machine."

This, if nothing else, penetrated her defenses. "How could you do that? Why? What if—?"

"I know what I'm doing," he said.

"Well, if you do, I wish you'd tell me."

"I plan to. Later. But we've got to see something first."

"I know you," she said, pointing an accusing finger. "You don't want him back—that's it—you want him dead."

For the first time, they were not speaking of Horatio. Jan could not avoid letting out some of the truth: "You're right." He stood up slowly and headed for the door. "Don't try following me. I want to be alone to think."

"You monster!" she screamed.

But that was all.

The problem was that Gail had not yet given up hope. When she did—when she finally realized that Kirk wasn't coming back, whether the machine was kept open or not—then she would be easier to deal with. But that might take time, he understood, and time was something they had very little of. When Gail admitted the truth, it also meant admitting that she had been an utter fool, and that, he knew, was what would take time.

By the time the machine had picked them up from 1849 and deposited them in the cave, he had figured out at least ninety percent of what was wrong. The rest —by sending Gail to the cabin to fetch the various volumes of the *Concise History*—had come soon after.

His theory still remained primarily guesswork. He hadn't dared voyage up the stream to attempt to confirm it through personal observation. That could be done later. But he believed he was right. The answer made sense—perhaps too much sense. It was like seeing the pieces of an apparently irreconcilable jigsaw puzzle fall suddenly and neatly into place.

There was horror in this—the terribleness of truth—but he had learned to bear that. Understanding, no matter how ugly, is always more beautiful than a lie.

But now that he knew, what was he supposed to do? So far he had taken no actions beyond a few defense measures: standing guard over the machine, shutting it down. But that was surely not enough. What else? What next?

He found himself walking through the forest that stood nearest to the cabin. Suddenly, the path he was following seemed too confining and he turned away and set off crosscountry. Eventually, a huge tree rose up to block his path. There seemed to be something irresistably inviting about the deep shade beneath it. He sat down on the soft moss and leaned his head against the wide trunk.

What would Horatio do if he were here now? That was really the significant question and the best Jan could manage was that Horatio would do what was right. But what was right? That was really what it all came down to.

He thought beneath that tree and perhaps he slept as well, for it was very nearly dark when he stood up at last and retraced his steps to the cabin.

When he entered, he found Gail seated in front of the fire, staring ambiguously into the spreading flames. She barely seemed to notice his return.

So, according to plan, he called out: "Gail—quick! Hurry! The cave! There's something you've got to see."

She sprang up. "Is it Kirk?"

He didn't intend to lie. To avoid doing so, he waved

131

frantically at the door, cried out again, "Hurry!" and dashed outside.

Of course, she came, too. In spite of his exhaustion, Jan led her a wild chase through the forest and up the slopes of the rocky hill. He beat her through the cave entrance by a full ten seconds.

She was panting and gasping when she joined him at last. A bright lantern illuminated the interior of the cave. Gail looked left and right, up and down, sideways and backward. She peered deeply into the darkest shadows.

Finally, she looked at Jan: "He's not here."

Jan pointed the musket barrel at her heart. "I never said he was. Now sit down. Over there. Sit."

Her eyes opened wide when she saw what he was doing. "Jan, are you crazy?"

"No, sane." He gestured with the musket. "Gail, move."

She went and sat where he had indicated—in the big chair among the time traveling equipment. Jan followed and pressed the appropriate button. In a moment, Gail was firmly latched in her seat.

"What are you doing?" she said, struggling vainly. "What are you trying to prove?"

"You'll see." He tapped the set of dials embedded in the arm of her chair. There were three. "Can you read these?"

"Of course," she said.

"And you know what they mean?"

"Yes."

"Then tell me what they say."

She laughed. "What's wrong? Can't you read?"

"Tell me," he said, sharply.

"It says Yellowstone, Wyoming," she said. "The first dial. And the next one says August 15, 1601. 2400 hours." She looked up. "But, Jan, that's silly. There was no one there then."

"Keep reading," he said tightly.

"It says—" she leaned forward against the straps,

132

stretching to see "—nothing." She dropped back. "You forgot to set them."

"No, I didn't."

"But if the second set is blank, it means that. . ." There was no need for her to finish the thought.

Jan was nodding in agreement. "That's right. It means you won't be brought back." He moved suddenly over and reached out for the activating lever.

"Jan, no!" she screamed.

He dropped his hand slowly. "I won't," he said. "I won't if you tell me the truth—and I mean all of it."

She was still strong enough to pretend ignorance. "What truth?"

He answered flatly. "About Kirk. What he did to time."

She failed to conceal her surprise. Well, at least she wouldn't be underestimating him again. And there was fear there, too. "I don't know what you're talking about."

"You don't have to lie to protect him. Can't you see what he's done? He's dumped you, Gail. He used you and now he's dumped you here to rot."

"That's a lie. You always were a liar. You always—"

"Then where is he?"

Petulant, almost mocking, she said, "How should I know? When he's ready, he'll come."

Jan reached for the lever. Gail screamed. Jan paused with his hand only inches away. "I'm not bluffing, Gail. I know what Kirk did. I know how. What I don't understand is why you let him. He killed Horatio. Can't you understand that much? He killed him."

"He did not." Her tone was less certain than her words. "Horatio was his friend. Kirk wouldn't harm him —unless he had to."

Jan struggled not to smirk. "Are you sure of that?"

"He told me."

This time Jan laughed.

"He did and he wouldn't lie," she said. "He knew what Horatio was doing and he thought it was wrong.

133

We both did. Changing time and making it go ways it was never meant to go. It just made me sick. We were manipulating them. Who gave us that right? All the history I had ever learned—it wasn't even true. And the corps—that was the biggest lie of all. So when we found out about the voyage to 1776, Kirk said it was our best opportunity. He said it was right at the beginning and if we could stop them there, then maybe it would mean we would stop them everywhere. He asked me to pretend I was mad at him so Horatio would have to pick him to go. But that was all I did."

"It was enough," Jan said.

"All he was going to do was talk to Horatio. That was all. I didn't see how it could harm things."

Jan moaned in disbelief. "Oh, no."

Gail glared angrily. "Don't be that way. I told you before Kirk wouldn't lie."

"Then where is he?"

"Somewhere. How should I know? He must have got trapped. Him and Horatio both."

"No," Jan said. "I don't believe that and neither do you. Horatio is dead and Kirk killed him."

"Why should he? If you know so much, tell me that."

"I don't know that," he admitted. But I have an idea. That's why we're here." Quickly, he came over and changed the settings of the dials upon her chair. Then he did the same to the other chair and sat down in it. The straps rose to enclose him. "We're going upstream to see if we can find out why." He had to assume she had told him everything. If he left her here, it would be even more risky than taking her along. He thought it incredible how easily Kirk had managed to sway and convince her. In a way, the idea made him very sad.

"I hope you plan on coming back."

"Look at your dials. What do they say?"

She laughed. "That again." But she looked, too. "They say July 18, 2169. But that's silly. That's today. Why do we want to go there?"

134

"To see if it's still there," said Jan, and he pressed the activating lever embedded in the side of his chair.

While Gail cried out sharply, the timevoid swept in and caught him up in its dark silent current.

CHAPTER FIFTEEN

"I never thought it could be like this," Gail said, nearly having to shout to be heard. She crouched deep in the ditch, her head shielded by her arms, while overhead the invisible helicopter continued to idle.

"I did," said Jan.

Suddenly, a stream of yellow light shot straight out from the side of the copter, painting a wide circle when it struck the ground in the adjoining cornfield beyond. Slowly, the circle of light began to move, up and down, up and down, crossing and recrossing the ditch.

"Jan, they'll find us," Gail said.

"Shut up."

"This is the wrong time. I know it's got to be."

"No, it isn't. The machine doesn't make mistakes like that. Now be quiet."

"But it's possible, isn't it?" The circle of light was coming steadily nearer.

"No." On an impulse, he gripped her hand and pressed reassuringly. "This is Iowa. July 18, 2169. Now hush."

"But—"

"Listen."

The helicopter was rising. They both could hear it. The loud whirring of the blades drifted away. The light was gone, too.

Gail didn't budge. "Did they see us?"

"I don't know—I hope not."

"But they were looking for us?"

Jan decided to gamble. He stood up in the ditch,

turned, and looked both ways. Around him the night was silent and empty. "They were looking for us."

"Was it those men in the town? The policemen?"

"If that's what they were, yes."

She stood up beside him, peering into the dark. "If they catch us, what will they do?"

"What do you think?" He climbed cautiously out of the ditch, then helped Gail up, too. He brushed fitfully at his clothes, scraping away the accumulated dust and dirt. He was glad there wasn't a moon tonight. The only light was the distant glimmer of the town far at the end of the straight dirt road.

"But this doesn't prove anything," Gail was insisting. "I mean, we don't know for certain Kirk planned it this way. How could he look into the future and know what would happen?"

"That's something I'd like to ask him myself."

"All he did—all that we know—he saved George Washington's army."

"It seems to have been enough."

"And this isn't the whole world. It's only one country, one part of one country. We don't know this wasn't here when we were."

"I knew. I lived here."

"Oh."

"But look over there." He pointed away into the corn-field. There, dimly through the darkness, a single vague light could be seen peeping between the black shadows of the cornstalks. "It must be a house. Come on—" he headed toward the fence "—let's take a look."

"Jan, no." She gripped his arm. "Haven't we seen enough?"

"I haven't. I came here to find some answers but so far all I've got is more questions. I need to talk to someone."

"But I hate it here. I'm afraid. I don't want to die—not here."

"It's where you were born." He tried, however, to

soften the impact of his word. "Come on. I'll take care of you."

"All right. I'm sorry if—if I'm not acting like a corpsman."

"Forget it. Come on." They moved together toward that faint light. Jan didn't want to seem too harsh on her. After all, what had happened in town—the suddenness and bleakness of the whole experience—it had shocked him, too.

They had arrived, as usual, in a vacant lot at the edge of town. From a first casual glance, the area seemed no different from any typical American agricultural settlement of the late twentieth or early twenty-first century. But this was supposed to be 2169, Jan forcefully reminded himself, and whatever this place was it wasn't a homestead village. They moved quickly into the town itself. At first glance, it, too, seemed quite ordinary, hardly the sinister place of Jan's worst imaginings. There had been a moment right there in the beginning when Jan might have admitted the possibility that he was wrong.

But the place was too quiet. That was the first thing that bothered him. He had timed the voyage to deposit them here shortly after five o'clock, when the town should have been at its most active. Yet the streets were empty of traffic—no vehicles, no pedestrians. Not a single store seemed to be open—the windows were dark, the interiors hidden in gloom.

He had set the machine for only a six-hour voyage. Because of that, fortunately, there was no need to seek shelter for the night. In any event, the one hotel they passed was also dark and closed. A hand-lettered sign claimed no vacancies were available, but the sign itself seemed very old and battered.

When a black, gasoline-driven car suddenly popped around a corner in the road, both Jan and Gail dropped immediately to the ground.

Why was that? Jan wondered, as he drew himself to his feet. The car was safely gone now. It was because of

139

the silence. The darkness. He had never felt so alone in his life.

"I don't like it here," Gail finally said. "There's something wrong. It's spooky."

"Did you notice anyone in that car?"

"No. Did you?"

He shook his head.

At last, near the end of the long central street of the town, they came upon a bar and restaurant and, through an open door, could see dim interior lights burning within. They paused and listened and heard the distant sound of laughing voices.

"Hungry?"

"No," Gail said. "But if you want to go in, I will, too."

"I think we should." But he didn't want to. He was nervous about what might lie through that open door; he was afraid.

Gail prodded him. "Come on—I don't want to wait." Her voice betrayed her own emotion.

Jan took a deep breath. "All right, I'm going."

Once past the open door, they followed a narrow corridor that eventually led them to the edge of a bright room. The place was filled with men. A wide bar ran the length of one wall and there were several wooden tables spaced here and there across the floor. All of the men were identically dressed. They wore black uniforms with black caps and each carried a pistol on his hip. The moment Jan and Gail emerged from the corridor, total silence seemed to descend upon the room. Even the noisy music box beside the bar stopped playing. Heads swiveled in unison and eyes glared.

Jan muttered, "Oh-oh," and started to back away.

"Hold it right there." One of the men at the bar stood up and came slowly toward Jan. He was big, huge, bar-rel-chested. "Do you have a reason for being here?" His right hand rested on the butt of his revolver.

"It was a mistake, sir," said Jan.

"Kind of a stupid mistake if you ask me."

Jan lowered his gaze to the floor and kept it fixed

140

there. "It's just that we saw the open door and came in-side. We didn't know it was your place."

"Isn't it rather late for taking a stroll?"

"Yes, sir. I suppose it is."

"Then look at me. I want to see your eyes."

"Yes, sir." Jan complied carefully. Of course, he pretended to be unable to meet the man's withering gaze.

"Now your identification papers." The man tugged at his gun to emphasis his request.

Jan shook his head sadly. "We left them at home, sir. I'm sorry."

Several more men had joined them now. Jan glanced furtively from one to another and was shocked by what he saw. These other faces were dead, stiff, frozen in place. A shiver crawled up his spine. Whatever they were, these things couldn't be human.

"Where is this home of yours?" asked the fat man. Of them all, only he was quite positively human.

"Outside town. My sister and I are visiting our aunt. We're from the East."

"In that case—" his hand didn't relax "—you'll have travel permits. Mind letting me see them? Or did you neglect to bring them, too? Another convenient mis-take?"

"Oh, no, sir," Jan said, having decided it was time to switch tactics from bluff to outright lie. "I have them both right here in my pocket." He reached down casually, moving in a painstaking way that attracted everyone's undivided attention. It was a trick Horatio had taught him. Then, just as he touched his pocket, he swung his hands suddenly up. Forming a big fist, he cracked the black-uniformed fat man squarely on the tip of his jaw.

Horatio had been a good teacher: the man folded at once.

"Run, Gail!" cried Jan. One of the other men had his gun out. As Gail darted away, Jan swung again. His fist connected cleanly but for all the affect it had on the man he might as well have used a feather. His knuckles stung fiercely.

Then Jan ran, too.

A single gunshot pursued him. The bullet dug a neat furrow along the corridor ceiling. Jan burst through the open door a few steps ahead of Gail and tugged at her to follow. They pounded along the concrete sidewalk, keeping deliberately near the shadowed storefronts. There wasn't time to turn and look and see if they were being followed.

Soon, they came to the edge of a dirt road. Jan stopped here, glanced back, saw nothing, then ran on. A mile from town, they came to the cornfield.

While they were standing there, the helicopter suddenly appeared in the sky.

Now Jan and Gail moved swiftly and silently between the tall rows of corn.

Soon enough, they reached the light they had been seeking and discovered that it came from a small white house. Gail suggested peeking through the curtained front window to see exactly who was inside. Jan said he thought that would be more risky than simply going boldly forward and knocking. "If they live way out here, I don't think they can be too dangerous."

"Well, I wish we'd brought the musket," Gail said. They moved softly onto the wide front porch and stepped toward a big green door. "I'd feel a lot safer with any gun."

"Next time we'll bring it," Jan promised. Actually, the corps was forbidden by regulations to carry weapons of any sort into the timestream unless they were common articles of attire in that particular time. But that couldn't matter now. Jan guessed that he and Gail were probably all that was left of the time corps. If his theory was correct, the others had either been wiped out or else left stranded in their hideaways. He was the Captain now himself and thus legally entitled to approve any special request. Like one calling for a gun.

Taking a deep breath, he tapped on the door.

A long silence followed. He was going to knock again when Gail suddenly jumped. Then he heard the footsteps, too. They came hesitantly toward the door.

Then a voice said, "Who is it? Please. We're friends here—good citizens. We haven't harmed anyone."

"We're friends, too," said Jan, trying to ease the fear he clearly detected in the voice. "Strangers."

"No, please. Please go away." This was a different voice—a woman's. In the background, Jan felt sure he heard a child whimpering.

Gail looked at him expectantly. Clearly, she felt he should make the decision.

He did. Though he hated to do it, he saw no good alternative to taking advantage of these people's fear. He slammed his shoulder hard against the door, then kicked out with both feet. "Open up in there! This is an order!"

Hesitantly, the door fluttered open. Jan rushed quickly through and Gail obediently followed.

Four people huddled inside the narrow hallway like prisoners awaiting execution. From the sound of their voices, Jan had expected someone older. Neither the man nor the woman was much past thirty. Both wore loose-fitting gray smocks and their heads were shaved nearly bald. The children, a boy and a girl, seven and five, reflected their parents' fear.

Jan kicked the door shut behind him.

The man was astonished. "You're not them."

"No," said Jan, "we're not. I told you we were friends."

"But what do you want here?" The man remained suspicious. "Do you want us to do something?"

"Only to talk. Just for a few minutes. Then we'll go and leave you alone. I promise you."

"But who are you?" This was the woman. Her voice was firmer and more in control than the man's.

"We're foreigners," Jan told her. "We want to know about your country. What it's like."

The man laughed bitterly. "Haven't you seen it?"

"Yes, but we want to know how it happened. What it was like before."

"Before what?"

"Before those things in the black suits took control."

This was a guess on Jan's part but it seemed to strike home. The man paled visibly at the mention of the black-uniformed men. Quickly, he said, "Why nothing happened, sir. We are each of us free and equal and very loyal to the——"

Jan shook him. No other technique seemed to work as well. "Don't lie to me. I told you I wasn't one of them. Didn't you hear the helicopter that was here a few minutes ago?"

"Yes, we did."

"We thought it brought you," the woman said.

Jan laughed. "That wasn't us—that was them. They were hunting us."

The man cried, "No!" deeply shocked.

But the woman seemed convinced. "Come in and sit down," she said. To her husband, she added, "We must trust someone."

He didn't seem so sure. The woman led Jan and Gail into a large room filled with old and battered furniture. They sat on a sagging couch and introduced themselves.

"I'm Myra Acton. This is my husband, Lawrence, and our children. If you want to ask us some questions, we'll try to answer."

"Then can you tell us how this came about? I suppose that has to be the first thing. And also how far does it extend? Just here? The entire state? The whole country?"

"I thought you said you were foreigners." This was Lawrence Acton, still not unsuspicious.

"We are."

"That's what puzzled me. Isn't it all the same?"

"You mean the whole world?"

"That's what the Watcher says."

"Who?"

144

Acton's eyelids narrowed to form tight slits. "You can't expect us to believe you've never heard of him."

"Maybe I should explain," said Jan, improvising rapidly. "You see, the country we come from is a very tiny land hidden in the high mountains between France and Spain. We have always been able to maintain our freedom and avoid outside control because there are only two mountain passes through which any enemy could attack us and these have always been very well guarded. We have no airfield, no train service, and even helicopters are kept away by unsteady winds." Of course, no such country existed but Jan guessed the Actons would not know that.

Apparently, they did not. Myra said, "Then the Watcher never got into your country?"

"No. I told you: we've never even heard of the Watcher. It was only very recently that we received news that awful events had occurred in the outside world. We are not callous people and so, in order to learn more, we began to monitor your news on television receivers." Jan spied such a set across from him in the living room. "What we saw greatly disturbed us and so my wife and I were sent forth to learn more."

"But how did you get all the way to Iowa?"

For the sake of verisimilitude, Gail answered: "We'd like to be able to tell you that, but you must understand it could be dangerous. For you as well as us."

"In each new place we visit," Jan said, "we try to start out as if we were completely ignorant, as if we'd just left our homeland."

"That seems a slow process to me," Acton said. "Why should you want to hear the same stuff again and again?"

"If the answers were always the same, it would be slow. But they're not."

"I see."

"Then would you please tell us everything you can."

Acton promised to try and, for the next hour, he and Myra shared the story between them. Jan and Gail learned that, some fifty years before, a man (or possibly

145

men) known only as the Watcher had seized political control of the known world. His power was centered in a massive police force composed of android soldiers artificially developed in former years to fight the apparently endless series of devastating wars which had long swept the world and made the Watcher's rise almost inevitable. The Watcher seemed to know everything. A man hardly felt secure in his own home. Millions had been murdered in the early years but that was no longer necessary, for obedience had been well established. The black-uniformed androids ruled every town and city. They lacked both mercy and restraint. If there was any way of escaping their tyranny, no man had as yet discovered it.

"Thank you," was all Jan could say when the story was finished. "You've been very patient and I want to thank you. But there are a few other points. When you were young and attending school, you must have learned some history, however distorted. Maybe you could tell us something about the past—about the shape of the world before the Watcher came."

"We know there were wars," Action said.

"Yes, but why? And who fought them? We have to know things like that."

Myra sighed loudly. "We may as well tell you the truth. Neither Lawrence or me has ever had a day of schooling in our lives. It's not authorized for farmers. We can't even read our own names."

"Then I suppose there's nothing you can tell me."

"Only what we already have."

But even Jan had to admit that was plenty. He stood up, motioned to Gail, and said, "Let's go." Their time was running short. They had to find a hiding place and wait for the trip home.

The Actons went with them to the front door. After saying good-bye, Jan and Gail darted outside.

The helicopter, fortunately, had not returned.

As they moved into the cornfield, Jan asked, "Well, what do you think?"

146

"We still don't know he caused this deliberately." She meant Kirk.

"No, but I'm not sure that really matters. It doesn't to the Actons."

"Then what do we do?"

"We have to change it back. Make time go right again."

"Can we?"

"I don't know. We have to try."

"But is there a way?"

"I don't know that, either."

It was very cold for both of them out there in that cornfield so far from home.

CHAPTER SIXTEEN

As soon as they reached the cabin, Jan climbed the rope ladder to the attic. Up here, he had a distinct feeling, he was most apt to find the one thing in creation he needed most at this very moment. If it existed anywhere, it was here. The attic was hot and the air clogged with dust. Breathing was not a simple process. In order to move, it was necessary for him to squat on his heels and shuffle from place to place. He maneuvered around the stacked piles of the *Concise History*, choosing to ignore them, at least for the moment, as too obvious. Instead, he uncovered a row of crates and boxes stacked against the rear wall. He looked carefully through them. He found heaps of old clothes, some letters, a bulky manuscript (someone's attempt at an epic poem), a few tapes, two rugs, curtains, a deerskin, and a great quantity of junk and clutter impossible to classify. Everything in the world seemed to be in these boxes in one form or another, everything except the one thing he was seeking.

But he found it. Needless to say, the last box he searched—the one stuck in the most secluded corner of the attic—was filled with books. His heart beat an extra stroke when he saw this. He went through the titles cautiously. There were novels, biographies, science, philosophy, religion, and a great deal of poetry, mostly in anthology form. None of the books looked as if they had been opened in decades. It wasn't until he reached the very bottom of the stack that he uncovered the one book he wanted. It was a single volume and the pages were even mustier than the others. Opening the book at random, he read a half-dozen brief paragraphs. Those were enough. This was indeed the book he wanted; he had guessed right.

The book was entitled, *The United States of America* —that was all. He glanced at the first page, then at the last. The story appeared to begin around the year 50,000 B.C. when the first human beings had come to the American continents; it ended in the year 2100, perhaps two decades prior to the emergence of the Watcher. In between these two dates, the story seemed both familiar and unfamiliar. In any event, it was not a story Jan had ever read before.

"What's that?" said Gail, suddenly crouched beside him. "Another history?"

"A different one." He closed the book and passed it to her.

She turned the volume in her hands. "It certainly doesn't look any different. Just older. What's so special about it?"

"Because it's our answer," he said. "This history is different because it's the real one."

After that, Jan was able to work exclusively from a theory. This was the same one he had first developed only days after what he now described as the cataclysm —the moment when time had changed. He let Gail work with him. She read the history book he had uncovered in the attic and agreed that it had to be so. For the moment at least, he chose to keep the explanation he had devised to himself. There was no need to make her feel worse than she already did. Not once after their return from 2169—the Watcher's World—had she asked him to activate the time traveling equipment in case Kirk was trying to reach them. He was beginning to think she might be coming to guess the truth, too.

His theory was not complex. It said simply that there were two histories. One of these was true and the other was false and the sad fact was that it was the false history into which he and Gail and everyone else he knew had been born. His own history—what he now called the Homestead World—was a lie. It had never really happened; it should never properly have been allowed to happen at all.

American history—this was the true one, the Watcher's World—included a successful Revolutionary War fought from 1775 to 1783. George Washington, the winning general in this war, was chosen six years later as the country's first President. In 1800, Jefferson had indeed been elected but he was by then third in the line of chief executives and not first. There had been no slave revolt in the 1850's. Instead, the festering sore of human slavery had been permitted to grow until, in the early sixties, a terrible Civil War had erupted between North and South, a conflict far more devastating than its counterpart in false history. In true history, Lincoln was a great war President, not a healer. There were other differences, too; the apparently minor ones —a different President elected, a new invention, an old face who did not exist—were far more prevalent than the really major ones. The whole thing culminated in a series of worldwide wars in the late twenty-first century and there, of course, was where history—at least in the form presented in *The United States of America*—came to an end. Jan knew the next part anyway. The final conclusion of the story. It was the Watcher.

Laying the two histories side-by-side, it was difficult to determine which, if either, was better or worse. And what about the rest of the world? He could only guess that it had not been directly interfered with but had been drastically altered in any event by the changes occurring in America. Still, the divergent endings of the two histories could not be ignored. If his own Homestead World had emerged new and better from the burnt-out husk of the old world, then in true history it was simply the old ugly world being superseded by a newer one that was even uglier.

Kirk had said the same, of course. Kirk had said the history serviced by the corps was a lie and now Jan knew this was so. More than that, he now believed that changing history was the primary goal of the corps: the rest, the research and scholars, was mere subterfuge. Time, as he saw it, was like a great river following the course it had followed through all eternity; it could not be easily deflected from this path. To prevent William Waite from meeting with his friend the Southern dandy, it was necessary to knock the dandy into a horse trough not once but rather to do it time and time again. And so the corps had been created to do just that—it was the only means by which the river of time could be prevented from returning to its natural banks. Then Kirk had interceded and with apparent ease had cracked the dams erected by the corps and true history was once more flowing effortlessly toward the sea. Now William Waite met with his Southern friend and together they devised the prototype for the later Native American party. So in Dallas, Texas, on November 22, 1963, a man named Oswald shot and killed the President of the United States from the sixth story window of a building overlooking the route of the President's motorcade. And so, in 1776, George Washington succeeded in evacuating his troops from Long Island and was not captured, tried, and killed.

But what about Kirk? Who was he and why had he acted as he had? Jan could only speculate. His opinions did not even deserve to be called theory. But this is what he thought: Kirk was a representative from that other time; he was one of the Watcher's men. Somehow he (and plainly others) had infiltrated the corps and then managed to manipulate himself into the choice assignment in the key locale so that, when the proper moment came, he was able to topple the first domino (General Washington) that set off the chain reaction that cracked the dam and sent time rushing back to fill its original course.

So his theory and speculations taken together succeeded in answering most of the basic questions of how and why. What was more difficult was deciding, what next? The simplest possibility—even Gail had suggested it—was traveling upstream to 1776 and making sure Washington was properly caught by the British.

But would that be enough? Or would it, like a twig thrust in the path of a tidal wave, be swept easily aside? To re-set the row of dominoes following the chain reaction it was necessary to replace all of them one-by-one—setting the first one upright was not enough.

He leaned against the outer wall of the cabin, watching a few clouds puffing listlessly through the sky. Overhead stood the noonday sun, its glinting rays bouncing brilliantly off the white Rocky peaks. Sometimes he thought it didn't matter much. These mountains, for instance, what did history mean to them? Real or unreal, true or false, they endured forever. Whether Washington was hanged or won a great war. Whether the Indians ruled America or the Chinese. No matter what, even if life had never come to Earth at all, these mountains would stand; this land would be the same.

But there were people here. And elsewhere. What about the Actons and their children? Didn't they deserve a chance to stand and live and breathe freely, the same as these dead hunks of dirt and rock and snow?

Jan thought, *yes*. And that was more than theory: that was faith.

He had to do something—for the Actons and for everyone.

But what?

Jan made a list. That night he gave it to Gail. He said, "I think this will do it."

She read the list carefully. There were exactly ten notations. "If it isn't enough, then what?"

"Then we try again."

She nodded and returned the list to him. "I see."

"You want to do it?"

"Yes, I do."

"Ten separate events in American history," he said. "Ten that we want to change back to their original

153

form. It may work—it may bring the homesteads back —and it may not."

"When do we go?"

"Dawn tomorrow."

She seemed startled. "That soon?"

"We've waited too long already."

"We had to wait. We didn't know what else to do."

"Now we know better."

She raised an eyebrow. "Do we?"

"Yes," said Jan, with what he hoped was certainty, "we do."

CHAPTER SEVENTEEN

It wasn't the same. Some things were similar, yes, but that only caused the differences to stand out more noticeably. The crowd, in particular, was not the same. There was a new, changed mood about it; a deep tension filled the air, a premonition— even an expectation —of impending violence.

This mood made him nervous in turn. Leaning over, he told Gail, "It's time. While I'm gone, whatever happens, don't move. Watch the crowd. If you see anybody who seems to be following me, anybody who tries to enter that building, then you'll have to take care of them."

"Who should I look for?"

"Anyone."

"And how should I stop them?"

He touched her coat pocket delicately. "If you have to, shoot. We'll be voyaging home in fifteen minutes. We're safe."

"But I can't just—"

"Yes, you can. You have to. Believe me, this is important."

She sighed. "I'll try."

It was November 22, 1963, shortly past noon. Dallas, Texas. For reasons of past familiarity, Jan had chosen to make his first attempt at changing time here.

He slipped swiftly into the crowd. Directly behind stood the building into which he had once seen Elinor Bateman disappear. He retraced her footsteps now. The elevator lifted him straight to the sixth floor. There he found the man with the gun. He was smoking quietly, watching the empty street below.

Jan said, "Freeze right there." He had his own gun out. Arriving here in Dallas an hour earlier than necessary, he had purchased a matching pair of .38 revolvers. There was no better place in all the timestream for purchasing weapons.

Jan came over and removed the man's rifle. He held it tightly in his left hand, the revolver in his right. "You're Oswald, I hope."

"How did you find me? Who told you?"

"Nobody," said Jan. "I want you to lay your right hand on the floor, palm up."

"Are you FBI? Police?"

"Just do what I say."

Oswald complied. Jan brought the rifle butt down hard across the knuckles. Oswald sprang up, howling in pain.

Jan backed off toward the elevator. "You won't be shooting any presidents now," he said.

Pausing at a lower floor, he dumped the rifle down a garbage chute. Outside, Gail ran up to greet him, her eyes wide with some unknown emotion.

He gripped her tightly. "What's wrong?"

"I thought I saw someone."

"They tried to follow me?"

"Yes. I mean, no. They started to but then they went away."

"Who were they? Describe them?"

"There was only one."

"Who? A man?"

"Yes."

"You didn't recognize him?"

"No. Of course not. Why should I? He was just a young man, with dark hair. He had on a big overcoat and it was hard to see him."

"Look around," said Jan. "You don't see him now, do you?"

She shook her head.

"Then we better get away from here. We'll be going back soon and we don't want to be too obvious."

"Then you did it?"

"No problem." They turned down a side street, seeking some obscure place from which to depart.

"Where next?"

"I think we ought to face it head-on," he said. "I mean, New York, 1776. It won't be as easy this time."

"No."

"You can't smash George Washington's knuckles with a gun butt."

"I know but I have an idea."

"Really? Well, tell me?"

"Later," she said.

He was glad to see that she had recovered.

They succeeded in getting inside the camp of the colonial American army with remarkable ease. Once there, Jan immediately enlisted as a recruit private, while Gail, displaying an unexpected talent at falsehood and flatteries, established herself in the officers' block. She said this fit in perfectly with her plan.

She had devised her own story, too. She said her father was Harold Wilkes, the owner of a huge rice plantation in South Carolina and a general in the state militia. In a few days, General Wilkes and a company of local boys would be appearing to join in the national struggle for freedom. In the meantime he had sent his daughter ahead to await his arrival and to alert Washington's army of his coming.

"And they really believed that?" said Jan, during one of the infrequent periods when they were able to meet and speak freely.

"Oh, sure," she said. "One man—a general, too— enormously fat—he said he remembered hearing of my father's exploits during the local Indian wars. They don't seem to even suspect that any pretty woman could ever be a spy."

"But pretty women make the best spies."

157

"Hush," said Gail. "You want them to hear that?"

It took Gail nearly a full week to implement her plan. Twice, they were picked up and returned to the cave and, after the second occasion, Jan set the dials for a stay of five full days. "We'll need at least that long," he said.

"Make it three days," said Gail.

"But—"

"Trust me."

He shrugged and did as she suggested.

As the second of the three days neared its end, Jan told Gail they might have to use desperate means. "I don't want to have to shoot the old buzzard, but how else are we going to get him out of the way?"

"They'll kill you before you get within six feet of him."

"I may have to try."

"Give me two more days."

"But—"

"Trust me, Jan."

Once more, he shrugged and said he would try.

Only a few hours after that, when he was standing near the end of a long line of men waiting to be fed, he glanced up and saw Gail passing. She was accompanied by a youthful, prim-looking major in a stiff blue uniform. Spotting Jan, she stopped and said, "Why, look over there, Major. It's Tom Holcomb if it's anyone." She was pointing at Jan.

"Who?" said the major, squinting with apparent disdain.

"Oh, I'm sorry," Gail said, "but young Tom was the overseer's boy on my father's plantation. He may have some knowledge of what has delayed them. Would you mind if I spoke with him? Only for a moment, I promise.

"Of course not." The major bowed stiffly. He offered to accompany Gail across the intervening few yards of muddy ground but she refused him politely.

Reaching Jan, she took him by the elbow and steered

158

him away from the line of men to a place where they would not be apt to be overheard.

"Your major is watching us like an eagle," Jan said.

"Let him. I came to tell you our plan and that's all right because the major is part of it. He knows I'm enlisting your aid in the conspiracy. I told him about you before."

"I give up," Jan said. "What conspiracy?"

"The one we're pulling tonight. The major happens to be one of General Washington's closest aides. They're like son and father, some say, though I can't verify that. So far, His Eminence—that's what they always call him—hasn't chosen to recognize my presence. But that isn't so important any more. The major will be our traitor."

"Why?" Jan couldn't believe it was going to turn out this easy.

"Oh, because he loves me, I guess. It's really too complicated to talk about. Come nine o'clock tonight, make sure you're standing by the guard post. The major will come with a horse. Then you'll both ride over and speak to the British. The major knows what to say— make sure he does."

"But that's all?"

"What else do you have in mind? Tomorrow the army moves out. The British will be waiting. *Boom, smack, bang.* Everybody's gone and the war's over. Washington gets hanged."

"But why should a patriot like the major want that?"

Gail smiled brilliantly. "Because he seems to want me even more."

Incredibly, it seemed to work as smoothly as the high notes of a pennywhistle.

Jan and Gail were among the few members of the colonial army to escape the British ambush. Jan had earlier found them a secure hiding place in a nearby briar patch. By mid-afternoon, they were safely huddled there. Gail had packed a lunch.

"Wasn't that easy?" she cried, chewing on a loaf of black bread. "Didn't I do everything just great?"

Jan told the truth: "You did wonderfully."

"I just wish we could stay and see him hanged."

Jan was shocked. "Washington? But why? You didn't used to be so bloodthirsty."

"Well, usually I'm not. It's just him—Washington— I finally met him. He's even worse than our books say."

"The other one—*The United States of America*— treats him like a god."

"Well, none of them tell the whole truth."

"And what's that?"

She whispered, as though the confidence was something too dreadful ever to be uttered aloud: "He wears false teeth. Wooden false teeth. And when he gets excited, they go *click, click, click*. Oh, Jan, you wouldn't believe how awful it is."

After four additional voyages up the stream, Jan said it was time to pause momentarily and rest and relax. Gail insisted she was prepared to go on but Jan said no. He counted on the tips of his fingers: "1963, 1775, 1929, 1858, 2097, and now 1972. I don't know about you, Gail, but if I pop into another new year I'm going to give up completely trying to figure out when and where I am."

"But you said we had to hurry."

"And we do. But there are limits. One free day— twenty-four tired little hours—that won't kill us. Besides, I've got to think."

So they decided to eat. For the occasion, Jan slew one of Horatio's fattest hens and cooked that with a few wilted ears of corn he had uncovered in the rapidly deteriorating garden. Gail agreed to make coffee. After dinner, they shared a cup.

By this time evening was descending upon the cabin. Jan started the fire and dropped down upon the hearth. Gail crawled up beside him and laid her head on his knees. "Where next?" she asked casually.

"1916 is next on the list. The last two voyages were tough and this should be easy in comparison. All we have to do is change the results of an election in which over eighteen million people voted. A snap."

"That was Hughes against Wilson, wasn't it?"

"Right, and in the new timestream Wilson wins."

"But we still get into the war. I remember reading that in your book."

"True, but Wilson gets us in earlier. And his rhetoric is different from Hughes'. We lose three times as many men in Europe and afterward there is a tremendous reaction to the Versailles Treaty, a return to strict isolationism. Because of that, the U.S. fails to enter the Second World War until nearly 1942. It's actually very complex."

"It's a mess," she said. "I remember in school how much I hated mathematics and this is just more of the same. You always have to keep so many different concepts going in your head at once. Sometimes I get the feeling that, after all this work, we're going to get to the end and find out nothing has changed."

"We can't think that."

"No, I suppose we can't."

They both fell silent then. The fire popped and flickered. Outside, a wind blew noisily.

After a time, Jan said, "Gail?"

Her voice reached him distantly. "Yes, Jan?"

"There's something I've been meaning to ask you."

"Sure."

"Remember on our first voyage? The one to 1963? When you thought you saw somebody trying to follow me? Well, since then, have you seen anything else like that?"

"No. Why? Have you?"

He shook his head.

"I was probably wrong that first time, too. Just imagining things. You know, the tension."

"Sure. That was probably it." But he didn't really think so. What bothered him was that nothing similar had happened since. Where were they? The Watcher's men? Surely, they hadn't given up—they had to be somewhere. Jan guessed they must be waiting. So far, he and Gail had only been lucky in avoiding them. It was a real miracle they had not met them in 1776. Presumably, the Watcher's men had chosen to disregard that moment as too obvious or else they had not yet had time to establish their best defenses. But that wouldn't be likely to happen again. No one's luck held out forever. At least four more voyages into the stream were necessary before victory became a genuine possibility. In that time, he was sure, they would meet their adversaries.

In 1916, Jan Jeroux and Gail Conrad, posing as a young married couple, registered at the Virginia Hotel in Long Beach, California. The Virginia was an ornate product of its own peculiarly garish age, but the rest of the world of Southern California that lay outside the windows of their room struck Jan as a puzzling place. It was too normal—that was the real problem—far removed from the crazy and yet also appealing Los Angeles he had visited several times with Horatio. Of course, the area's boom years still lay largely in the future. He couldn't very well blame Kirk for this particular change. From their room, it was possible to see the skeleton derricks of a half-dozen oil wells rising from the nearby hills. This pleased Jan more; it was better. These were the harbingers, he thought, certain symbolic evocations of the world that was to come. These wells and, not far from here, the whirring cameras of young Hollywood. It was coming—a new kind of world—and nobody could stop it.

But all of that was rather beside the problem of the moment. Jan had come up with what he hoped was a simple and direct plan for winning the necessary change in this era. It was why they were registered at this particular hotel in this particular city at this time. He went straight to the telephone, picked it up, and asked the operator to connect him with another room.

At this moment, the Virginia Hotel housed two of the biggest figures in American politics. One, Justice Charles Evans Hughes, was the current Republican candidate for the Presidency. The other, Hiram Johnson, was Governor of California. Although both belonged to the progressive wing of Republicanism, Johnson had so far refused, out of stubborn envy, to endorse Hughes's candidacy. According to *The United States of America,* this refusal—strengthened by a supposed snub suffered by Johnson at Hughes's hand in this very hotel—would inevitably lead to the defeat of Hughes in heavily Republican California by the margin of 4300 votes. As a result, Woodrow Wilson would be reelected President of the United States in November, 1916.

So Jan placed his call to Hughes' hotel room. Amazingly, he was able to reach Hughes' private secretary. He was becoming as good a liar as Gail.

"Hello," he said, "this is Governor Johnson's secretary and I'm calling in behalf of the Governor who would very much like to have a meeting with Justice Hughes."

As expected, the secretary lunged at the bait. "Why, of course. When and where?"

"In your rooms. At your convenience."

The secretary excused himself briefly. When he returned, his voice was even brighter than before. "Will one o'clock be possible?"

"It will be fine," said Jan.

"Then Justice Hughes will be pleased to receive the Governor."

"Thank you very much." Jan replaced the phone, immediately picked it up, and asked for another in-house number. This time he announced himself as Justice Hughes' private secretary.

He was soon speaking directly to Hiram Johnson.

"Sir, Justice Hughes has requested that I call and

163

invite you to join him today at one for lunch in his rooms."

Johnson's reply came swiftly: "I'm afraid I have another appointment at that time."

"But, sir, can't it be—?"

"It's a very important appointment, young man."

"Well, so is this, sir. You see—" Gail, beside him, was gesturing frantically for the phone. Unable to think of anything convincing himself, Jan passed her the receiver.

She said, in an incredibly authoritative voice, "What seems to be the problem here?"

Jan heard a sharp though indecipherable reply.

Gail said, "But I'm sure that can be cleared up. I'll be down to see you in two minutes."

Another shrill burst of sound.

"Of course. I'm sure it won't take long. We're all busy, sir. Good-bye."

Hanging up the phone, she rubbed her chin pensively.

"Well, what did he say?"

"He told me to get lost."

"But you can't—"

"Nope." She was already heading for the door. "Look them in the eye," she muttered. "Didn't Horatio always say that? Look them in the eye and they'll never lie to you." She shrugged. "Well, maybe they can't say no, either."

Then, with a wink, she went out.

Twenty minutes later Gail returned with another wink. "He said yes," she said, flopping on the bed and staring up at the ceiling. "I knew it. Men were so chivalrous in these days. He didn't dare tell me to go to hell, yet it was the only way I was going to go. Finally, when he realized that, he had to say yes."

"You're gorgeous," Jan told her.

"And smart, too. So is Johnson. When I explained the facts of the matter, it helped. All I did was tell him in so many words—and knowing it was true must have made it sound true to him—that Hughes couldn't win without his support. If Hughes did win, then he would owe Johnson a monstrous dept of gratitude. He would have to reward him in one way or another. After all, if you can't be in the White House yourself, what's the next best thing but having a friend in there? Woodrow Wilson wasn't anyone's friend. Johnson finally understood that."

"But what happens when he discovers Hughes has never heard of you?"

"Well, if we're lucky, he won't even ask. If we aren't, I don't know, but I bet he won't walk out."

"Let's hope so, but we'd better be realistic. We really ought to get out of here before someone sees us. We've got the rest of the day till we go home. I think we better find another place to hole up. If Hughes and Johnson get to comparing notes, they may trace us here."

"If they do, we can always say we thought they were somebody else."

"Sure," said Jan, who was already packing. "Now get over here and help me."

The suitcases were stuffed with old books, of course. But Gail helped.

When Jan told the clerk at the desk that he and Gail were leaving now, the man peered down the length of his nose and said, "I'm going to charge you for the entire day."

"Okay," said Jan.

"And in the future I'd like to suggest you take your business elsewhere. There are several nearby establishments that will gladly cater to your peculiar needs."

Getting the point, Jan glared angrily but it would have been useless to protest. Narrow minds knew only narrow thoughts and this clerk looked to be about as narrow as a skinny toothpick. Through tight lips, Jan paid his bill, then led Gail toward the door. He could feel the desk clerk's disapproving gaze following them all the way.

Just as he and Gail were about to step through the front door and into the street, a flash of sudden sideways motion caught his eye. Swiveling slightly, Jan glanced behind.

Crouched on a knee halfway between the desk and the door was a man. Jan knew him. It was Kirk Rayburn.

"Get down!" Jan cried, knocking Gail to the floor.

The bullet smashed into the glass door in front of them. Its apparent trajectory exactly matched the place where Gail's head had been only a bare moment before. Jan reached into his vest, but before he could draw, Kirk was on his way. He dashed past the astonished desk clerk and vaulted up the winding staircase, taking the steps two and three at a time.

Jan helped Gail to her feet. "You're all right?"

"Yes. Thanks. I think you saved my life."

Two husky men in dark suits had raced up the staircase in pursuit of Kirk but one was already coming back empty handed.

The desk clerk fluttered over to Jan. "Who was that man? I know he wasn't registered here. I'll swear by that. I never set eyes on him till he drew that weapon."

"A thief," Jan explained decisively.

"But it looked like he was trying to kill you. On purpose."

"Well, some thieves do that. When it's the only way to get the money they really want."

"But you never saw him before?"

"Never in my life."

"Or—" the clerk glanced meaningfully toward Gail.

"Or her, either." Gail clung to his arm. Jan held her sternly upright.

The clerk still seemed far from convinced, but Jan didn't care. He wanted to hear what the two detectives had to say about Kirk.

"He got clean away," one of them told the clerk. "Disappeared right on the fourth floor landing."

"He probably ducked into a room," Jan said. "What you ought to do is organize a search." He was searching himself now—it seemed the right time for devising a means of getting himself and Gail out of here. "Look into every room."

The clerk was horrified by the conception. "Here? At the Virginia? Why, that's impossible. Our clientele. Why, Governor Johnson himself is here right now, And Justice Hughes."

"Why, I bet that's it," Jan said. "That man was an assassin. He mistook me for one of them. You'd better get your men upstairs right now. Hurry."

The urgency in Jan's tone was enough to convince the clerk. He ordered the detectives racing upstairs.

Once they were gone, Jan took Gail and headed for the street.

The clerk pursued. "Wait—hold on. Shouldn't we notify the police? If this man is an assassin, they have to know."

Jan paused and laid a hand on the clerk's shoulder. He spoke softly. "Do you think that's wise? The publicity? I'm sure your men are capable of handling the situation. Quietly."

"Yes, sir."

"Then we hardly need the police, do we?"

"Oh, no, sir."

"Fine."

On the street, Jan told Gail, "Well, we won that round."

She nodded vaguely.

"Is something wrong?" So far she had given no definite indication of having recognized Kirk.

"Later," she said. "Can we talk about it later?"

"Of course."

Jan found them a clean room in a considerably less ornate hotel. They had until midnight to wait. Jan paced the room in nervous anxiety. After the excitement of the day, he was growing bored.

"We ought to do something," he said, "to keep from going nuts."

"What?" she asked, in a flat voice.

"Well, how about a movie? They're a lot of fun in these years. Charlie Chaplin and all that. There's one called *Intolerance* I noticed playing uptown and that's supposed to be very good."

Gail shook her head stiffly. "I don't think so."

"Well, we could just see the sights. Take a streetcar to the beach. We've never really had a chance to do that."

But Gail again said no.

Jan sat down beside her on the lumpy bed. "All right," he said. "If it's really as bad as that, then maybe we better talk it out. Right now. Just tell me exactly what's bothering you."

"Him."

"Who?"

"The man who tried to kill me. That was Kirk, wasn't it?"

"You saw him?"

"Enough to recognize him. And I think I saw him that other time, too."

"He was the man in 1963? The one you thought was following me?"

"I couldn't be sure."

"Well, it was him this time."

"Then it must have been him the other time, too." She was holding back her tears. He watched her lip quivering. "Jan," she finally managed, "can you tell me why?"

He told her—everything—the entire story. There was no longer any reason for holding back. Gail was strong enough now to bear the truth.

She waited until he finished before saying a word. Then she said, "So it was just a lie. How about that?

Every damn bit of it. Kirk used me. He's one of those horrible men. He works for the Watcher."

"He must, though he is human. After a fashion."

"And he fooled me. Without me, nothing would have changed."

"Well, he fooled me, too. And Horatio."

"Not in the same way."

"No. It wasn't the same." He didn't intend to lie.

Gail simply nodded. After a time, she got up, went to the bathroom, and when she came back, her face was clean and scrubbed.

"Let's go to that movie now."

Jan sprang up. "Fine."

On the way to the theater, watching every passing face with caution, Jan told her, "This won't be easy. We can never be sure where they'll be. If they've caught us twice, chances are good they'll catch us again. It may not be so easy for us the next time."

"But they can't change it back, can they? I mean, once we've succeeded in a time, they can't go and ruin our work."

"Not right away, no. I'm sure of that. They'd have to wait for our change to fade. That's what Kirk did with Horatio. They have to stop us before we can act."

"And we can't let them do that."

"No."

The movie was indeed an excellent one.

By the time they arrived back home, Jan had made up his mind: it was time to take the initiative. He based his decision upon a principle Horatio had often advocated: that any strong offense was better than a weak defense. He also had usually added, "And it gets you killed quicker, too."

So Jan sat in front of the fire with Gail curled up like a kitten at his feet and said, "The only way we can beat them is to meet them head-on if necessary and win that way."

169

"I agree. But how? We don't go upstream to the Watcher's own time again, do we?"

"No. That would be fighting them on their own ground and I don't want to do that. I think I've found the best place, though it won't be much easier."

"Where?"

"Not where, when. One of the few moments in American history when the individual actions of one particular man really affected the entire course of future history. I noticed it immediately as soon as I began to compare our history with theirs. It was a perfect time to work a change, but I also realized they would know that as well as me. I'm sure they have a strong force waiting for us there. It's why I didn't include it on our list of ten. But now I think it's where we've got to go next."

"Well, what is it? Stop being so secretive."

"It's the invention of the cotton gin. By a man named Eli Whitney. In 1793."

Her face fell. "You're kidding."

"Nope. Just think of it, Gail. A workable cotton gin in 1793. Consider the possibilities. It would revolutionize the practice of slave agriculture. Lead to the creation of giant cotton plantations from Carolina to East Texas. I swear that half the major divergences between the two timespring from this one event. There's the Civil War, the lack of a slave uprising, the war over Texas, the failure of the South to industrialize. I could make up a list as long as your arm."

"And you want to stop it?"

"Yes. The way I see it now, the cotton gin is such a consequential event that to prevent it from happening, along with everything else we've done, might just be enough. If we can do this, we may have beat them."

"So they'll stop at nothing to stop us."

"No, so we can't go right away. That one history book isn't enough, either. The stuff about Eli Whitney is very sketchy. We'll have to research his life further. Find the significant moment to stop it."

"How long will that take?"

"A day or two at the minimum. We'll have to voyage upstream and read some books."

"Then that's what we'll do," she said, with definite certainty.

"We must." Leaning over, Jan kissed her forehead gently.

CHAPTER EIGHTEEN

Jan spent two full days in the New York City Library in September of 1975. When he emerged, he felt he knew all that could be known of Eli Whitney and the invention of the cotton gin.

Whitney had graduated from Yale College in September 1792—after nine years of study—and was soon turned down for the teaching post he had expected in New York. More out of desperation than anything else—Whitney had a closet full of bad debts and such men were tossed in prison in those years—he then accepted an offer to tutor the children of a certain South Carolina plantation owner named Major Dupont.

Whitney set sail for the South but his ship ran aground and he was forced to return to New York out the price of passage. Once there, he came into contact with a smallpox victim and was forced to remain in the city, undergoing variolation treatment, which consisted of a series of inoculations taken from the blood of mild sufferers of the disease.

Whitney recovered. In the meantime, through the agent of his future employer, he struck up a friendship with Catherine Greene, the wealthy widow of a famous hero of the Revolution. Mrs. Greene also owned a Southern plantation—hers was in Georgia—and she loaned Whitney enough money for him to again book passage to Savannah. Mrs. Greene would also be journeying home on that same ship. During the course of the voyage, Mrs. Greene invited Whitney to visit her plantation and spend a few days before continuing on to South Carolina and his job with Major Dupont. He accepted. Not particularly eager to assume his new duties, Whitney extended his brief stay into a long vacation. While there, he learned of the apparently insurmountable difficulty faced by Southern planters in trying to extract the seeds from upland cotton. Inspired, Whitney immediately set out to develop a means for doing this. Within six months, he had invented a workable cotton gin. As a result, he never did go to South Carolina.

Studying this narrative, Jan could easily spot several key moments in Whitney's history where intervention seemed most apt.

Back home, over dinner, he informed Gail of his decision. "We'll go to New York. I think it's better than waiting for him to go South."

"But won't they think so, too? Kirk, I mean."

"I imagine so. But that's the point. We can't be afraid to meet them face-to-face. Besides, I bet they have Whitney shadowed from the day he was born until the moment he finished work on the gin."

"Then they're sure to spot us."

"The idea is we spot them first."

"There is one point that bothers me, though. I thought, in 1776, we took care of the Revolution. But now this woman—Mrs. Greene—you say her dead husband was a famous general in the war and that's how she got her plantation. The land was a gift from the state of Georgia in honor of General Greene. So the way I see it is: no war, no general, no plantation. Therefore, Whitney cannot invent the cotton gin because there's no place for him to do it. Right?"

Jan shook his head. "Wrong. You see, the changes have to be cumulative. It's like the ripples that form on the surface of a pool when a stone is dropped in the middle. They spread outward, growing wider all the time. Well, so far those ripples we've made have not extended as far as 1792. And they won't, either—unless we drop another stone."

"By blocking the cotton gin?"

"That's right."

"Then when do we leave?"

"Dawn tomorrow."

She grinned. "I'll be ready."

In 1792, New York City was a tiny, grim heap of a town with a population still numbering in the thousands. Livestock, including hogs and hens, roamed freely through its muddy boulevards and stagnant pools of water lay against the curbs in dark, dank profusion. The odors of garbage and sewage clung everywhere.

Jan was glad the Academy had inoculated them against every known contagious disease. In these foul streets there must be a hundred to catch.

They rented a room as husband and wife in a comfortable Dutch inn. A tavern was located on the bottom floor and, their first night, Jan left Gail in the room and went down to mingle with the natives. Nobody claimed to have heard of any Eli Whitney, which wasn't especially surprising, but Jan did meet a man, a one-legged veteran of the war, who told him that, yes, Catherine Greene, the general's widow, was indeed staying in the city. "She was heading back home when her ship ran aground on the rocks below Hell Gate. Now she'll have to wait and try again."

"I've always admired General Greene tremendously," Jan said, attempting to explain his interest in the widow. "I'm glad to hear she came to no harm."

"Ain't you a shade young to have fought in the war?" The veteran appeared to think it impossible for any civilian to have an interest.

"I am, but my father fought. Under General Greene's command."

"I stood under Arnold myself. Fought at bloody Saratoga, which is where this was lost." He flapped the vacant leg of his long trousers. "For the honor of my country."

Jan knew little of Saratoga, which did not exist in the Homestead World. "Arnold, yes—a great fighting man."

175

"And a bloody traitor." The veteran glared with suspicion.

"Of course," Jan backtracked. "I didn't mean to imply otherwise."

"A good general, anyway," the veteran agreed. "A pity he never learned which side was rightly his. Why, if I had him here with me today, I'd tell him that, too." He chuckled. "Then I'd hang him."

"Only what he deserves," Jan murmured, wanting very much to get away from this bloodthirsty old soldier.

"Hang all traitors!" the man suddenly cried.

The following morning, shortly after dawn, Jan ventured out alone to reconnoiter the downtown inns and hotels. He posed as a newspaper reporter and told the various clerks that he was looking for Catherine Greene. Finally, at one singularly luxurious establishment, he found her registered.

The clerk, a dapper little man with a stiff English accent, told how she had returned a few nights past after her terrible ordeal at Hell Gate.

"Do you know if she'll be available later in the day? I'd like to interview her for my paper. About her late husband."

"Well, there's a pair of other gentlemen with her at the moment."

This worried Jan. "Could you describe them? Is one a thin, dark man, with side whiskers? A Mr. Eli Whitney of Connecticut?"

"I don't know the name but that sounds like one of them."

"Then I ought not to disturb her now." Jan started for the door, his mission accomplished, then suddenly turned back. He asked the clerk, "Is there another way out of here? Out the back?"

The clerk frowned. "Why do you want that?"

"Competition. Other reporters. They follow me everywhere. Worse than leeches. They'll suck you dry if you let them."

176

The clerk showed mild sympathy. "I suppose that's a problem in your line of trade."

Jan laid a gold piece on the counter. He pretended not to be aware that it was there. "In fact," he went on, "if somebody should come after I leave and ask if I've been here, I wish you'd say it was somebody else. Tell them I was looking for a room but decided not to take it. Don't mention Mrs. Greene. If they describe me, say it's somebody else."

The gold piece swiftly disappeared from view. The clerk bowed smartly. "Glad to be of any assistance."

Jan nodded and then followed the clerk's careful directions through the dark innards of the hotel. He emerged into a muddy alleyway and moved stealthily down its length. He had nearly reached the corner when, from behind, someone shouted, "Hey, Jan Jeroux. Hey, there."

He continued walking as if he hadn't heard but, the moment he turned the corner, he started running as fast as he could. The next alleyway he reached, he darted down it. He hopped a fence, dropped into someone's yard, avoided a large dog, and finally reached a familiar street.

From there, he hurried back to the inn.

He told Gail he had located Mrs. Greene.

"Any trouble?"

"A lot. Kirk was there."

"He saw you?"

"Yes, but from a distance. I pretended not to know him and got away before he could get closer." He told her more of the recognition and his subsequent flight.

"Then they can't be sure it was you."

"But they can make a good guess."

"So what do we do now?"

"The way I see it is this way. Whitney will have to stay in New York at least two weeks to undergo treatment for smallpox. There's no way he can leave the city before then. Therefore, what we have to do in the interim is convince Mrs. Greene to leave instead. That way, Whitney can't go with her and thus he's never invited to her plantation. Also, we have to do it in such a way there's no chance of anyone changing her mind and getting her to come back here."

"Is there any way of doing all that?"

Jan nodded. "At least one way. But it'll take time. Not our time, but hers. I think we should give them at least four days. Her and Whitney. We want them to be very close before we move in to split them apart. Four days, then we move."

"And until then?"

"We stay here. We stay hidden. And we keep our guns handy—just in case."

"That won't be easy. Waiting."

"It never is. But we can start by having dinner. I understand the local Dutch cooking is superb."

"You're on," she said.

Four days following Jan's first visit to the hotel where Mrs. Greene was staying, a pair of strange figures approached the same building from the alleyway that ran behind it. One of these figures was a stooped, heavily black-bearded man, who walked falteringly with the aid of a cane. A woman accompanied him, equally decrepit and dressed in clothing that seemed to have been stitched together out of discarded rags. The man seemed nervous and apprehensive. As he shuffled through the mud, he often turned, glancing behind. One hand was shoved out of sight in the folds of his torn coat.

At last, the two entered the hotel through a rear door. As soon as they were inside, the man stood straight up, dropped his cane on the floor, and stripped off his black beard. He then handed the woman a clean cloth.

"Get rid of as much of the dirt as you can. The old clothes and the gray hair will do just fine."

"They should help convince her I'm telling the truth."

"They nearly convince me."

When the hotel desk clerk spied Jan and Gail

approaching from behind, he gave a quick, surprised jump.

"Don't you remember me?" Jan asked.

"Yes. Of course. The reporter." He seemed as nervous as Jan ten minutes before.

"Don't let these clothes fool you. I only wear them to keep the competition from spotting me on the street." He laid a gold coin on the counter. "I'd like to see Mrs. Greene if I may."

"Well, you're in luck," the clerk said, with a heartiness that was obviously false.

"How so?"

"You caught her alone. Her friend— the one you asked me about—caught the pox. He still comes around often but he's out being treated now."

"He won't be back for a while?"

"You just missed him." The clerk was staring at Gail with a puzzled expression.

"Oh, this is my secretary," Jan said. "She takes down dictation."

"Well, you can go up if you wish. Mrs. Greene is in room seventeen, top of the stairs, go left."

"Anybody been around here asking about me since the other time I was here?"

The clerk shook his head definitely. "Not a soul."

"I'm glad to hear that." Jan laid another coin on the counter; the first had mysteriously disappeared. "Thanks for your trouble."

"You're very welcome."

Jan led Gail upstairs. They passed the first landing and continued up another flight of steps.

"I thought he said it was down there," Gail said. "Room seventeen."

"He did, but last time I was here I got a look at the register. Mrs. Greene is in twenty-four."

"Then you think—"

"I think something stinks rotten," Jan confirmed.

When the second landing came into view, Jan cautioned Gail to be silent, gestured her to stay put, then crept slowly to the head of the stairs. Peeking down the hallway, he saw a lone man standing in such a way that it was clear he had no business being where he was. Jan estimated he was standing beside the door to room twenty-four.

He hurried back to Gail and warned her to keep watch on the stairs. Then, as carefully as possible, he replaced the thick beard he had worn through the streets. "How do I look?" he asked, when it seemed snugly in place.

"Oh, you're beautiful," she said.

Jan nodded and started off. When he reached the landing, he drew his gun from his belt and shoved it down into a coat pocket. He kept his hand tightly wrapped around the butt. As he started down the hallway, he whistled shrilly to himself. The man standing there stared at him. Jan couldn't know if he was being recognized. He was only twenty feet away. Then ten. He kept whistling, attracting the man's attention without arousing his suspicion.

At least that was what the theory said. But, just then, a sudden light of recognition dawned in the man's eyes. His hand fell toward his waist. Jan drew out his gun. The man was drawing, too. Jan saw no other choice. He cocked his wrist and, with all the might he possessed, hurled the gun straight at the man's head.

As quickly as it had deserted him, his luck returned. The gun smacked solidly against the man's forehead. He toppled without uttering so much as a moan or whimper.

Jan hurried ahead. Tearing the man's shirt into long strips, Jan tied his wrists and legs. Then he made a gag.

He ran back to Gail and told her what had happened.

"Now what?" she asked.

"We have to go through with it." He drew her up the stairs until they stood beside the body.

"What are you going to do with him?"

"I'll drag him down with me. The way I see it, room seventeen has to be a trap. There's probably a bunch of them in there waiting for us to stumble in. I want to keep an eye on the door to make sure they stay there."

"Don't shoot anyone."

"No, not yet. We don't want an uproar. I just hope nobody innocent wanders by till I'm ready."

"But you want me to go in?"

Jan nodded. "Right now."

He sat the unconscious man on the stairs and dropped his own coat over the man's shoulders to cover his bound wrists. The effect was that of a passed-out drunk.

Jan then accompanied Gail to the door of room twenty-four. He signalled her to knock. When she did, a voice from inside called out: "Eli, is that you?"

Gail said, "I've come to see you about him, Mrs. Greene."

There was a pause. Then: "Who are you please?"

Jan nodded sharply and, in response, Gail emitted a long low moan. Her voice was pleading. "Please, Mrs. Greene. You must let me in. Oh, please."

That seemed to be enough, for the door popped immediately open. Jan drew back into the shadows where he couldn't be seen.

He heard Mrs. Greene say, "Why, my dear, whatever is it?"

"I must talk with you," Gail said breathlessly. "Please. It's urgent. You must believe me."

"Why, of course I do. Please come in. Now what did you say—?"

The door shut here.

With this part out of the way, Jan felt he could breathe more easily. He went for the stairs, found the man no less unconscious than before, and pulled him quickly down to the first floor landing. Then he bundled him up as before and dropped down beside him. When a pair of strangers came past, Jan pretended to be suitably drunk. He laid his fingers across his lips and muttered, in a wavering voice, "Please 'scuse my friend here. He's got to sleep to be beautiful."

181

The strangers—a man and his wife—looked properly revolted.

As soon as they had gone, Jan drew out his gun, then proceeded to wait.

As expected, not sixty seconds passed before the tentative head of the desk clerk peeped around the first corner below.

Jan pointed his gun right there. "Move an inch and I'll blow it off."

The clerk gulped, unable to find any words worth speaking.

"Come up here and stand beside me," Jan ordered.

The clerk came obediently. He told Jan, accusingly, "You're not a newspaper reporter. Those men told me. You're a crook."

"So are they. How many are there in there?" He indicated, down the hallway, room seventeen.

"Three men, I believe."

"Do you have a key that'll lock that door from the outside, so they can't open it from the inside?"

"Of course I do." It seemed to be a point of pride. Two more guests—a man and wife—came downstairs. Jan tucked his gun in his pocket. The clerk appeared to consider calling out for help. Jan shook his pocket meaningfully. The clerk had second thoughts. Except for some curious stares and a murmured, "Disgusting," from the woman, the couple passed uneventfully.

"Where is that key?" Jan asked.

"In my pocket, of course."

"Then go down there, don't make a sound, and lock that door. Then come back here." The gun was out again. "One false peep and I go *boom*."

The clerk did exactly as directed.

When he returned, Jan said, "Can they get out a window?"

"If they're willing to jump twenty feet."

"I imagine they are. What I want you to do, if anyone else comes by who isn't involved in this, say you've sent for a constable to arrest us." The unconscious man

182

continued to breathe harshly. Jan didn't think he'd be waking up for a while yet. "If they are involved, I suggest you get out of the way fast and stay there. I ought to ask for my money back, too."

Waiting proved next to unendurable. Jan expected at any moment to be rushed from below but nothing happened. Fortunately, the staircase remained largely deserted. Only one couple—a young man and woman — passed and they appeared far more interested in one another than in any drunks.

Finally, Gail appeared from behind. She was beaming like a cat who has swallowed a fish. "It was beautiful," she told Jan. "Mrs. Greene believed every word I told her."

"You're positive it was enough?"

"She told me she would leave directions that Mr. Whitney should not be allowed upstairs. She even offered to intervene with him in my behalf but I said he had ruined me and was too callous to care. She accepted that without protest, so I guess their love hasn't run too deep."

"She'll leave with him?"

"She said she'd be taking tomorrow's stage to Boston. A ship will be leaving there for Savannah in a few days. Oh, and she also gave me five hundred dollars to tide me and the baby over. I couldn't refuse. What should we do with it?"

"Give it to Whitney if we could. He'll need it now. Gail, do you realize this means it's all over?"

"We've beat them?"

"Yes, but you almost sound sad."

"Maybe I am—almost. It was fun."

He nodded, stood up, and rapped the clerk cleanly over the head with the butt of his gun.

He pointed downstairs. "Let's go."

"We can't wait?"

"Not that long. The machine won't pick us up till midnight tomorrow. We've got to get out of here now, one way or another."

183

"We could jump out a window."

"And present clear targets. No, they'll be waiting in the streets. We have to meet them head-on."

She shrugged, drew her gun out of the folds of her gown, and started down.

Jan caught up with her and moved ahead.

He was the one who peeked around the corner into the lobby. He counted four men there. One was behind the desk and another behind a couch. The other two were crouched down beside the door. Fortunately, there was very little cover in the lobby.

Because of that, Jan was able to hit both the men beside the door before anyone had time to return his fire. The wall beside his head burst into splinters. He ducked back.

"A good start," he told Gail, "but there'll be more in the street."

"We aren't going to get out of here, are we?"

"I doubt it."

From above, he could hear the sound of something hard being smashed against a wooden door.

"Room seventeen," he told her.

Again, he tried to dart around the corner and get off a shot but the instant he exposed himself the return fire drove him back.

"I think it's impossible," he said.

"Still just two of them?"

"Yes."

"Maybe we ought to rush them—both of us."

"I don't—" The sound of a breaking door from the floor above was enough to convince him. If he was going to die, he wanted it to come cleanly and not from being trapped. "You aim at the couch. I'll take the desk. Reload now and we'll each have eight shots. Keep firing and run as hard as you ever have."

"Run where?"

"Let's try for the desk. I'm sure that's Kirk back there. If we can take him with us, the trip'll be half worthwhile."

"But we've won," she said. "We can't forget that."

"No."

"There's glory in our defeat."

"No, in our victory."

Footsteps sounded from behind. A bullet bounced off the ceiling overhead, sending splinters raining down. Jan jumped out first, firing at the desk. Gail came right afterward. The man behind the couch tried to sneak out. Gail's first bullet cut him down. Then they both concentrated on the desk. There was no way Kirk, hiding back there, could expose himself to fire. Jan was almost there, Gail not too far behind. Then a figure appeared in the doorway and fired from there. He was a good shot. Gail screamed and slid over.

Jan stopped and spun. Bullets were whizzing all around. He wanted to go back, but the blood pouring from her breast convinced him that was pointless.

So he fired his last shot at the desk, threw away the gun, and vaulted over the top.

Kirk was right there waiting for him. He threw up his hands in defense. Jan knocked them aside and got a firm hold on his neck. He squeezed. "I'm going to kill you right now. I'm going to squeeze the life out of you."

Kirk whimpered in fear. Jan could hear the others running. He squeezed harder, wanting to get this done before it was all over for him.

Then the room faded. The whole world seemed to pitch and sway and grow dim.

Then the void of the timestream swept forward and engulfed him within its deep, unique blackness.

He held on to Kirk's neck. Together, they fell through the void. Jan wept with relief. Kirk silently screamed. Jan held him tight, refusing to let go.

Then the cave was around him. He blinked into a glaring light. He tried to say something but couldn't.

"I see you brought me a present," said an oddly familiar voice.

Jan stared in astonishment.

185

Standing in front of him, as real and big as life, was a dead man.

Horatio Nextor.

Right then, Jan must have passed out.

CHAPTER NINETEEN

"Well," said Horatio Nextor, "how's it feel to be alive?"

Jan blinked furiously at the illusion that hovered over him, but the thing refused to go away.

"Don't go and pinch yourself," Horatio cautioned. "I'm real enough. You ain't dreaming any more."

"But you can't be real."

"Sure, I can." Jan was becoming slowly aware of his surroundings. He seemed to be lying in a bed in the central room of the cabin. He noticed another bed, across the room, with someone else in it.

"Who is—?" he managed.

"It's her," Horatio confirmed. "Gail."

"But she can't—"

Horatio laughed. "You sure seem eager to bury all your friends in their graves. Gail's alive and so am I. You, too, for that matter. As for Gail, I thought she was a goner when I pulled her body out of that chair. It was touch-and-go all last night, too. This morning, she woke up not much less chipper than a hummingbird. We talked for a while, then I put her back to sleep. It would've been a whole lot easier, though, if you hadn't also saddled me with a sneaky prisoner."

"You mean Kirk?"

Horatio jerked his head toward the front door. "Got him tied in the yard. I keep hoping a grizzly will wander by and make a meal of him, but the last time I checked he was still all there. How come you decided to bring him back? Gail missed that part and couldn't tell me."

Jan shrugged. "I guess I'm not really sure myself."

Horatio nodded. "No harm in that. There's little enough real mercy in this universe without voting against what little of it does appear. Besides, Gail came up with a good idea what we should do with him. She's merciful, too. She says we should hold a trial, find him guilty as charged, then exile him back to around a hundred thousand B.C. I like that idea myself."

"Then you must mean . . . you mean we actually did it? Time is right again."

"Wrong again, actually, but you know that part. In fact, when Gail told me how much you did know, I was more than a mite embarrassed. I knew you two were good, but it's plain now you were better than me. After all, I was the one who let Kirk lure him into 1776, where I got jumped by seven blacksuits."

"Then you knew about Kirk all along?"

"Well, we had our suspicions. The way those three—all good corpsmen—died in Tibet, that smelled poorly. We guessed, if Kirk was a spy, he must be trying for a transfer. So we gave him one to smoke him out, sent him here. Everybody figured I could handle him. Well, I couldn't."

This brought Jan's mind back to something that had been bothering him since the beginning. "Horatio, why aren't you dead?"

"A fair question. But I'll tell you. The main reason is because Kirk and his partners didn't kill me. They must have known they didn't have to, because I was already dead to begin with. You see, I was born into real history, into the Watcher's World. I was a physicist and worked for the government. So did Gail's grandfather and several other men, including the most brilliant of the bunch, Sidney Lackland. We didn't do much. Few governments have much use for scientific research unless they need weapons and the Watcher didn't, because he already ran the world. So Lackland came up with the calculations for the time traveling process. He told the few of us he could trust. We all tinkered on it together. Pretty soon, say in fifteen years, we had a machine. We played around with that. I don't think any of us expected anything to come of such a crazy notion. But it worked. We changed time. Not all at once, but bit by bit over the years. By the time the Watcher caught on to what we were doing, his world was nearly gone. They came after us. I was caught and killed. Never mind the details, but it wasn't fun, and if anyone ever tells you that when you're dead you're dead and it doesn't matter how you got there, you tell them Horatio Nextor, who knows, says that isn't so. But the others got away and they did what they set out to do. Time was changed and—guess what?—in the new world born of this tampering Horatio Nextor turned out to be alive, after all. The corps was founded. Lackland himself was the first Captain. We figured it would be fun, exciting, educational, and also the best way of preserving what we had accomplished. What we didn't know—what we do know now thanks to Kirk—is that some of the Watcher's men had escaped. They had apparently infiltrated our ranks. They waited fifty years to move. Kirk tells me his father was one of these. He hid out on a Homestead, brainwashed his son into dreams of power, and finally sent him to where he could do us some harm. I've relayed all of this to the Academy. Hopefully, we'll get them all this time."

"So when time was changed back, then you were dead again?"

"That's right."

"Then I saved your life. Sort of."

"You saved it, with no sort of."

"And you were really dead? Twice?"

"That I surely was. I told you when we first met that I'd seen a few things nobody else ever has. That's one of them: the land of the dead."

"But what—?"

"Nope," he said flatly. "Don't even ask. There isn't a man alive who won't eventually be dead. Who am I to tell all the answers so soon? It would be the same as spoiling a good mystery by revealing the solution in the first chapter. Wait till you reach the last page, Jan. Then you'll know, too."

But Jan was trying to wave his hand. He was pointing toward the other bed. Gail's eyes were open. She was watching them now and she seemed to be smiling.

Horatio stood up. "I'm going out now," he said. "It's Kirk's feeding time. I'll be back in a half-hour or so."

"A half-hour?" Jan said. He was looking at Gail. Their eyes were locked and there seemed no need to speak.

"He's a slow eater."

"Do you think he might ever take a whole hour?"

Horatio laughed. "I'll see that he does." Turning, he went toward the door.

Then Jan stood up. His knees wobbled awfully and his head spun as he crossed the room.

But he didn't fall.